Stallion Shield

Guardians of Chaos 3

C.D. Gorri

Stallion Shield

Guardians of Chaos Book 3
by C.D. Gorri
Edited by BookNookNuts
Copyright 2021, 2022 C.D. Gorri, NJ

To creative chaos everywhere, keep on doing what you're doing…

STOP! Before you go, sign up for my newsletter and get the latest on my releases, giveaways, freebies and more:
SUBSCRIBE HERE

Description

He knows she's his mate, but this stubborn kitchen Witch isn't making things easy.

Furio Lo Duca is a Stallion Shifter with serious problem. Set in his ways, the Guardian has a reputation for being tough as nails, but a certain kitchen Witch sees straight through to the heart of things. Will he continue to fight his destiny? With Loyalists threatening to disrupt the balance of magic, the Guardians must pull together. They need to be at their strongest.

Can this Jersey boy claim the sassy, smart-mouthed Jessenia, taking his rightful place among his team, or will self-doubt destroy all he's worked for?

Guardians of Chaos Pledge

I am the watcher in the storm.
I am the sword who strikes true.
I am the iron shield.
I protect against those who seek to control the wild
nature of magic.
I am the guardian of chaos.
To thrive, we must be free.
From chaos comes creation.

Prologue

Chop, chop. Scrape, scrape. Place in bowl. And repeat.

Jessenia smiled for her followers as she demonstrated the proper way to choose, clean, and prep fresh herbs for her latest delectable recipe. It was difficult to concentrate when she had so many things crowding in on her already full mind, but she muddled through. Cooking was her jam and vlogging both her successes and failures was how she paid the bills.

Putting together dishes based on her experiences with cuisine from across multiple cultures, and new cooking fads had always brought her a sense of peace and purpose. Jessenia supposed it was a good thing she was trained to be a kitchen Witch.

Her powers really seemed to shine when she was brewing potions and healing salves. And she was getting better at both every day since she'd started living at the Keep and taking lessons from Holley.

Of course, thinking about Holley made her think of Furio, and that led to even more complicated emotions. It was an eye-opening experience for the young American kitchen Witch. Holley was able to bring her knowledge of the past and both her European and Native American cultures to the present. Jessenia was grateful for any knowledge she imparted to her. Heck, she was happy just to be allowed in the door.

"Whoops," she stopped and plucked a stem from the sprig of thyme she'd been stripping out of her pile of herbs, "You want to make sure you don't rush this step. There's nothing worse than biting into a hard, wiry stem from a thyme plant," she smiled, already feeling her cheeks heat up with embarrassment.

But that was nothing new. She'd polled her audience early on in her vlogging endeavors, and it seemed they loved she could admit her mistakes to them. To err was a very human trait, she supposed, and was glad her followers knew she understood that.

Perfection was not her goal. In fact, Jessenia

often emphasized the opposite on her show. She wanted folks to know that cooking was messy, but awesome fun. Recipes should be fluid and based on what was accessible to the chef in their own home arena.

"Remember, any fresh herbs will work for this souffle," she smiled, listing various combinations that went well together as she worked.

Where the careful cleaning and preparation of the herbs for this dish might have seemed like a boring waste of time back when she'd been a young Witch, Jessenia had come a long way since then.

She used to follow her poor Nana Carol around like a little lost kitten back in the day. Tugging on the older woman's apron strings while she snacked on whatever yummy goodness her grandmother had been preparing, bombarding her with mountains of questions at the same time.

Gosh, she had been so annoying back then. She shook her head at the memories with a momentary self-indulgence. And yet, her Nana had always had infinite patience with her. The older Witch had taught her so much before she'd passed far too soon in Jessenia's opinion.

Memories of her childhood warmed her almost as much as the superb quadruple ovens in the Keep's superb, restaurant quality kitchen. All of the appliances were in exquisite condition, and better yet, they were on some kind of magical warranty. In other words, they were entirely self-cleaning.

Sigh. That alone was worth moving in for, but really, it had seemed natural in the heat of the moment. With Fergie gone, the apartment they had shared was just too costly. Besides, she was there all the time.

She worried her lower lip as she added the herbs and shredded cheese to the egg mixture, showing the audience as she went. Yes, she loved it there, and yet Jessenia had been doubting her decision to live inside the Keep just recently. Pushing the thought aside, Jessenia tried to focus on the task at hand.

"There, now we fold this in with our other ingredients. Doesn't that smell great?" she smiled and breathed in the herb scented air.

Tilting the stainless-steel mixing bowl, she whisked the contents to a froth. Technique was something a chef developed, and she had hers down. But the people watching her were not trained in culinary arts, they were regular people, and it was her job to make recipes like this accessible and less frightening.

"Okay, this is the big payoff for all that hard work

peeling the leaves off the thyme, and quadruple rinsing the sand off the basil and parsley. You see, this requires patience, but in just a few minutes the results will prove worth it," she winked at the camera and continued to whip the mixture for her *light-as-air* ricotta and herb souffle.

Her weekly vlog was important to her. It not only provided her with enough money to maintain her old truck and chip in for food and things in the Keep, but it was her way of connecting with people.

"Okay, just pour it into your ramekins like this. Now, who is ready for the results? Check this out."

Setting aside the mixture, she opened the oven. Jessenia always had a finished product waiting to show her followers since cooking in real-time took actual time that neither she nor her viewers had. The fragrant souffle filled the kitchen with a delightful aroma, and she pulled it out carefully with her oven mitts on, lifting it to show her online audience.

A flurry of hearts and thumbs-up emojis flooded her screen, and gratification filled her. Jessenia's vlog currently had over one-hundred-thousand followers, and her sponsors were thrilled with her steady progress.

Still small time, for sure, but she was happy. And that counted for a lot these days, given the fact her emotions were in constant upheaval. How could they not be when she was being driven crazy by an arrogant, cocky male who thought he was above all reproach?

Furio Do Luca was the bane of her existence. He'd not only made life difficult for her mentor and newest best friend, Holley, but he spent most of his time either staring at her like she was some damn science experiment or ignoring her.

The jerk. Still, he was pretty darn cute, and he had the nicest ass she had ever seen. Perfectly muscled and rounded, her hands itched to give it a slap every time he walked by.

What? She had eyes, and they worked. The man was hot. Even if he was an arrogant jerk face, it didn't lesson her attraction to him. Jessenia was still allowed to look and appreciate. So, what if she wasn't exactly talking to him at the moment? It did not detract from his good looks.

A shame. Yeah, right. Sniff. Whatever.

She could judge herself to death later. Right then, she had to concentrate on her audience. Making good, home-cooked food less scary for folks was kinda her thing.

So? Jessenia loved food and wanted to share that

love with the world. Growing up with working parents, she absolutely hated the way they'd grabbed fast-food almost every night instead of cooking for her and themselves. Like a real family did at least once in a while.

Her grandmother was the total opposite, and she'd loved the older woman to pieces. She'd passed on her love of food to her granddaughter, which only grew once she'd inherited her powers, and embraced her kitchen Witch heritage.

Whoever said chicken soup was a cure all had no idea. It totally was. The ritual of cleaning, preparing, chopping, and adding ingredients was highly ritualized. Good cooks knew this. That was why they had their favorites.

Favorite knives, cutting boards, pots, pans, utensils. All of it was based in Witchcraft, though normals denied its existence. It was part of who she was, and she wanted to bring that sort of holistic approach to tackling kitchen tasks to her followers as well.

Just imagine being able to ease the mind and body through comfort food readily prepared at home. Jessenia understood the convenience of eating takeout. Heck, it wasn't like she never grabbed a hot dog or burger on the run. She just wanted people to know cooking wasn't half as scary as it seemed. Anyone could do it.

"And there you have it," she smiled and presented the perfectly golden souffle, "Remember folks, magic can happen in any kitchen. Even yours."

The back door to the kitchen slammed open, and she suddenly stopped filming. With a click of a button, she switched on the usual credits and the jingle she'd prepared for the end of the show.

Nerves fluttered around her stomach. How irritating! She ignored those pesky butterflies and began to clear away her mess as the group of Guardians, whose kitchen and home she'd recently invaded, ambled in from their recent scouting mission.

"Something smells good," a familiar voice called out.

Eeek! It was *him*. The only man in the entire manse who could set her heart to pounding like she'd just run a hundred-yard dash.

Furio. The youngest Shifter in the bunch, he was still decades older than her. Not that he looked it. The man shared his body and soul with his equine half, a Draft Horse, she'd learned in passing.

He was absolutely gorgeous with his long, dark hair, emerald eyes, and olive-toned skin. His Italian heritage evident in his Roman nose, and tendency to use traditionally recognized Italian American colloquialisms in his speech.

He entered the room, and she stopped like a deer in headlights. His lips curled, and she recalled the movement meant something different to Horse Shifters than a mere smile. He was tasting the air, testing the atmosphere.

Shit. She only hoped her body didn't betray her feelings. Turning quickly to see to the oven, she worked hard to ignore his presence. Some secrets had to be kept for a reason, she reminded herself. Hardening her resolve, she stopped her heart's foolery before it could run away with her.

He is not for you. She told herself and went back to getting lunch on the table.

Chapter One

"Hey Jessenia, you cookin' in here?" Storm called and pulled himself up short before he could bump straight into Furio's back.

He'd recognized the Wolf's voice and knew he was simply being friendly. Shifters were always hungry, but Furio still did not like the idea of his buddy being so casual with Jessenia.

The female in question turned and grinned. Not at him. No, never at him. The warm, wide smile was for Storm. That just made him want to punch the fucker in the gut. She'd probably be pissed if he did that.

With a heavy sigh, he refrained and stalked past her to the dining room. It was getting to the point where he could hardly walk into the room without getting all growly and pissed. But that was what happened when you denied yourself, he supposed. Having Jessenia so close but being unable to claim her was wreaking havoc with his emotions.

Unable? The fuck you say, his Stallion snorted. The beast was more than able. And he assured his human half of that little fact.

Shut the fuck up. He gritted his teeth and talked down his baser side. Not that he didn't want her or could not claim her. Actually, it was pretty fucking complicated. After the morning they'd just had, he didn't want to think about it.

"Lunch is ready," her voice broke the blissful silence that had settled on his mind, and he winced.

Not because he did not like her voice. On the contrary. He liked it far too much. Spent many a restless night imaging her using it to call his name.

Mincha! That's all he needed. A fucking hard on at the table. He growled again, but an elbow hit his arm and he met Storm's confused stare.

"Dude?"

"What?"

"Nothin'," the man shrugged, "This looks great, Jess," he said warmly.

Furio allowed himself to look across the table,

and his chest squeezed. The mostly vegetarian meal she'd prepared, with the help of the Keep, comprised almost all his favorite things. He didn't know if she did that on purpose or not, but it touched him either way.

She knew the home where they all lived was magical. Knew the kitchen would present him with a vegetarian option had she made meat for the rest of the group, but it was almost as if she wanted to cook for him. No one had ever done that before, and it touched him deeply.

Tell her, the Stallion pushed. Furio ignored the pesky Horse and grabbed a fork. Next, he reached for one of the steaming ramekins, which cooled by the time his fingers grabbed it.

The *manetuwak*, or the spirits of the Keep, as Holley called them, liked to take care of the inhabitants of the residence. She was their resident Witch/Shaman and mated to their Alpha, a Diamond Dragon named Kingston.

She was also the reason everyone was walking on eggshells around him. Totally his fault. He knew that. His Stallion was pissed as hell at him because of the bad way he'd handled his Alpha mating the Witch.

Now that Jessenia was currently studying under

Holley, she probably hated him too. He didn't blame her at all, but it was one more reason he could never tell her the truth about what she meant to him.

Pain lanced his heart, and the delicious meal turned to dust in his mouth. Still, he kept eating, acting nonchalant. He'd even joked with the others, though he could tell they were more reticent with him than normal. It had been that way for months now.

"This is so good," Fergie said to Jessenia, and everyone echoed the sentiment.

Everyone but him. He could hardly look at her, much less tell her that her food was amazing. He felt Storm frowning at him, but he kept his head down and went through the motions of eating. Same as he had for months now.

Hell, it was all he could do. Work, eat, sleep, and repeat. Like he was stuck in his version of *Groundhog's Day* hell. Unable to confess to the woman he loved what she meant to him. Unworthy of her in every way.

Fucking hell, he stood up and brought his dish to the sink. He needed to go work out or something. Anything to get away from the sweet heavenly scent of her. A Guardian should always be in top form, he figured, and headed for the training room.

Thoughts plagued him of the night when all his hopes for the future had gone sour. He'd been looking for Jessenia and had finally tracked her down in the old library.

No one else was around, and his sweet, curvy *piccolina* was curled up on the chaise reading one ancient book or other. Furio was not a big reader. Hell, he hardly passed school, but it wasn't because he was stupid. Hardly.

Kingston would never allow any ward of his to be anything other than educated. Furio simply preferred action to more intellectual pursuits. He liked running, playing guitar, and sparring. He also liked fucking. What could he say? Ever since he was a teenager, he knew it was something he was exceptionally good at it.

But ever since he'd seen the little kitchen Witch something had gone wrong inside of him. Furio was not interested in sex with anyone else. Hell, his Stallion went nuts if he even thought about it.

No two ways about it, she was different. Special even. And he wanted her.

"Whatcha doin' there by yourself?"

He stalked over to her and gave her a slow grin that had melted the panties off many a female in his day.

Jessenia had barely glanced his way. Lifting her big, brown eyes a fraction, she'd returned them to the page she'd been studying just as quickly.

"Reading," she replied.

"I know something else we could do that's more fun," he tried again.

"Are you serious? Do you really think that line is going to work with me?"

"Hey, I know you're just as curious as I am."

"How would you know that? You've never even tried to talk to me."

"Talkin' is only one way to communicate," he said, "I know others."

"I bet you do, Mr. Italian Stallion, but you don't know me," she said, "and you have no idea what I want or need."

"Piccolina, I know I got what you need right here," he growled.

Chest heaving, he crossed the room, more than able to meet her challenge. Placing his hands on either side of her head, he mashed his mouth to hers. Stealing a kiss that rocked his entire fucking world for the first time. Like ever.

"No," she pulled back, "We can't do this. I can't do this. Not after the way you treated Holley."

"What does she have to do with us?" he asked, utterly confused.

He knew the little kitchen Witch wanted him. Hell, he wanted her too. And he thought he'd proved himself by being part of the effort to retrieve Holley from Offner's clutches.

"She is my friend, Furio, and you made her feel unwelcomed here," Jessenia shook her head sadly, "I just, I can't do this," she pushed past him, rushing out of the library leaving her book on the chaise.

Furio had fucked up. Apparently, he'd been wrong in thinking that his mate wanted him back with just as much heat and surety as he'd wanted her.

Thank fuck, he'd kept that little tidbit of information to himself. Rejection was a familiar if unwanted emotion in his lifetime.

Fuck if he'd give anyone another opportunity to do so formally. No, he would keep the fact she was his mate to himself.

It was safer that way.

Chapter Two

Lunch had started off so promising. And yet, as Jessenia watched Furio stalk away, the mood had turned decidedly sour in her opinion.

The Guardians of Chaos did not exactly advertise. They were an organization made up of groups of elite supernaturals. She only knew about it for two reasons. One, she was a Witch. Two, her BFF was mated to a Guardian.

Fergie had been kidnapped by the Loyalist's a few months ago and Jessenia met up with the group to get her back. She would do anything for her bestie. That much hasn't changed, though a lot of other things had.

"So, what's cookin'?"

Speak of the devil. She turned to see Fergie wagging her eyebrows at her. Jessenia had to squint at the redhead's newest fashion ensemble. Her bestie was a fan of red despite her orangey locks. She wore a clinging red wrap-around dress and, of course, a pair of spiky silver heels. Her choice in footwear made Jessenia cringe when she thought about taking a step in those things.

Hell to the no. More of a combat boot in the winter, flip-flops in the summer kinda gal, Jessenia shook her head and pointed at the table. Her best friend's obsession with high-end footwear was unhealthy, in her not-so-humble opinion. Detrimental was another word that came to mind.

The last time she wore heels she was at her senior prom, and she'd kept them on all of two minutes before slipping on a pair of ankle socks and rocking out to *Nirvana* with Sergio, her best guy friend *evah.* The Jersey Bull was one hell of a dancer. Like someone took genes from Fred Astaire, the Jacksons, and John Travolta and made one badass Shifter cocktail.

Hmm. What was with her and hoof-footed Shifters with Italian heritages, anyway? Not that she ever had the hots for Sergio, but Furio, well that was another story.

Jessenia wanted the Stallion with every fiber of her being. Once upon a time, she'd thought he'd returned that interest, but after she'd turned him down after one passionate kiss, he hadn't tried again.

Maybe she should've went for it when he'd given her the chance. But Jessenia didn't do casual sex. It wasn't how she was built. If the stories Fergie's mate had imparted about the Stallion were true, then she'd gotten away easy.

The man was a heartbreaker. Collecting notches on his bedpost was a way of life, and she could never be just that. Not even for him.

"Smells wonderful, Jessenia," Kingston nodded his customary polite greeting, jarring her from her unpleasant reverie.

The Alpha of the Group and a Dragon Shifter, Kingston was enormous. The tallest, widest, and perhaps scariest fucker there. At least, Jessenia thought he was. Which was saying something, considering they had a Vampire in residence.

Then again, she kind of liked the mysterious Vamp. Hell, she liked all of them. Byram was nothing if not courteous to her in an old-world sort of way she found charming. Egros, a male Witch whose specialty was portals, was a bit more standoffish, but she was used to that kind of thing from other Witches.

Many supernaturals paid little mind to her or her kind. They thought a mere kitchen Witch beneath them. That was cool with her. She just ignored them right back.

"I'll fetch Holley, and we will join you in a moment," Kingston announced, clearly communicating with his mate via their special telepathic link that only bonded mates could afford.

The interaction was so amazing to watch, though it made her feel slightly voyeuristic. Jessenia smiled sadly. Would she ever have that? Would her mate search for her with eyes blazing?

She could only hope and dream, she supposed. As it was, Holley beat him to the punch. The tiny Witch came hunting for her mate in the dining room before he had time to stand. Three months swollen with their young, Holley was either in a tizzy of energy or asleep.

She'd taken to napping most mornings as her pregnancy kept her up during the night. Or Kingston did. Either way, she was not resting now.

"Hello," she smiled.

"Mate," he seemed to breathe the word as she nuzzled his lips with hers.

It was their customary greeting, and Jessenia stopped and averted her gaze. She realized she was staring, and that wasn't exactly cool. Crap. She really needed a life of her own.

But the truth was, Holley's pregnancy was another reason Jessenia was in residence. Everyone worried about the Alpha's tiny mate wearing herself out, so Jessenia stayed to help with things. Like the preparations for the herb garden.

Cooking and taking care of the Keep was her pleasure. She wanted to learn from Holley, and if that meant lightening the expectant mother's load, then she was only too happy to help.

"So, you make any meat for us carnivores?" Fergie growled a bit, eyes flashing as they romanced over the many veggies and sides she'd prepared.

Jessenia rolled her eyes. She'd never get used to Fergie's new Wolfish side, she supposed.

"Of course," she said, and nodded to the tray that seemed to be one of the Keep's favorite.

Sitting beside a smaller tray full of individual ricotta-herb souffles that were each identical to the one she'd prepared for her vlog, *courtesy of the Keep,* was a huge rack of lamb beautifully cooked with rosemary and garlic. Fergie sighed and began to load her plate while Jessenia opted for a souffle.

"Thanks," she murmured when Storm handed her a bowl of fresh spring greens she'd made into a salad.

She set the bowl down and sighed. She'd made it for *him*. Of course, Furio had eaten and gone before she had a chance to even catch her breath, much less offer him any.

The dang Stallion was driving her bonkers. Usually, she could tell the second he'd left a room, but he'd snuck in and out in record speed this time.

"Good?" she asked and waited a beat for Fergie to sample the salad before she went back to her meat.

"Yeah, but Jess, you know I'm carnivorously inclined these days," she said and nodded towards the corridor where Furio had disappeared, "So. I was wondering if anything has happened on that front yet? Ow!"

Jessenia grunted when Fergie's elbow connected with her side, causing her to drop her fork. Thank goodness the rest of the Guardians were engaged in their own conversations and no one was paying them any mind.

"Ow," Jessenia grunted, "How many times do I have to tell you, you are stronger now?"

"Sorry! My bad," Fergie snorted, and opened a

covered platter that suddenly appeared on the table in front of her.

Jessenia frowned. Beef enchiladas in red sauce? Sometimes, the Keep was just plain nosy, she thought. At least the darn magical manse could stick with the menu. *Ugh.*

"Mexican? Yes!"

"Are you seriously going to eat that after that lamb you just put away?"

"What? I'm a growing she-Wolf, right babe" the insufferable redhead winked at her mate, whose growled answer was incomprehensible to the kitchen Witch.

Thank God, she shook her head and sighed again. Those two were a little too much with their PDAs. Fergie barked a reply, *like really barked,* then tossed her head back and shouted to the *manetuwak.*

"Thanks, Keep!"

"I still can't believe you identified the Keep as a magical entity before everyone else here," Jessenia shook her head and grabbed the glass bottle of home-made salad dressing she'd made.

It was a simple vinaigrette with some mustard seed and honey, but the fresh herbs made all the difference. She was leaning more towards vegetarian just lately and knowing the reason made her chomp the lettuce a little more roughly than she normally would have.

Oh well, she sighed. It wasn't like the greens had feelings. Not like she did anyway.

"Same," Fergie was already munching her second enchilada happily and agreeing with Jessenia's heartfelt sentiment.

She loved her friend, but the woman was hardly what she would've called empathetic only a few months prior. But that quality only grew as she got to know her mate and her Wolfish side better. It was wondrous and new, and Jessenia was happy for her. Really.

Okay, maybe she was a tad envious, but that would never get in the way of their friendship. They'd been through too much for that. Lunch at the Keep, like most mealtimes, was busy and noisy one minute, then over the next.

Jessenia mused at how quickly the food went, as did the people. Before finding their fated mates, the Guardians ate most meals on the run, though some were prepared magically by the Keep. Yes, the castle did a good job. The food was wholesome, but this was different. This was family.

"I am going to take my mate to bed. She needs her rest. Thank you again for lunch, Jessenia,"

Kingston said before standing and picking his mate off the floor princess-style.

"What is that?" Storm looked at Furio's half-eaten ramekin skeptically.

"A souffle," she said.

"Is it vegetarian?"

"Yes. No meat. Eggs, cheese, and herbs."

"Sounds like Furio's favorites, I wonder why he left it," he said, then grunted when Fergie's elbow connected with his ribs.

"Shh," her bestie growled.

Jessenia grinned, mildly amused at the byplay. Yes, he'd tried it. And yes, he left it half-way through. Maybe he just did not care for her cooking. She shrugged and ate her own food. The Stallion was so not her business.

"No, I meant, uh, it smells incredible," Storm turned a deep shade of red and smiled at his mate carefully.

"Thanks," she murmured, looking look at her own plate and not the two of them.

Would they ever stop tripping over the elephant, or in this case *horse*, in the room? Probably not.

"Look, Jess, I know he's rough, but give him time," Storm said, his hand clasping Fergie's.

Jessenia did not know what to think. Did

everyone know she pined for the man? Shit. Even Fergie looked ready to beg on his behalf.

"Guys, there is absolutely nothing going on between me and Furio. I don't have to give him a chance to do anything."

"But I thought-"

"Well, you thought wrong. Excuse me," she stood up and cleared her place.

Dammit. She needed to work on hiding how she felt. Especially in a room full of supernaturals. Things had been strained ever since he'd objected, and loudly, to Holley's presence. It wasn't that he disliked the Witch. It was more that he felt disloyal to the memory of Kingston's fallen mate.

Jessenia was there the day the Alpha had told his sorry tale. Neela was not a mate in the traditional sense. Kingston had explained the circumstances of their mating in painful detail, and Jessenia's heart ached for them both. But Holley was the Dragon's fated mate, his *conpar*, and she completed him in a way the she-Dragon never could.

Jessenia hardly recognized Furio when he'd lashed out. It was like a bus -sized bug had crawled up his ass and died whenever Holley was concerned.

Oh sure, he'd come around. Eventually. He'd even defended her from the Gila Shifters working with that crazy ass Warlock. But he obviously had hang-ups. Besides, he'd made it abundantly clear that she meant nothing to him.

Jessenia would just have to get over her annoying little attraction to the man. That wasn't going to be hard. Right? She only liked him a little. Very little.

Yeah. Right. Okay, fine, so she wanted to jump him, but she refrained. Playing it close to the chest, as it were.

Not that it matters, she reminded her inner Witch. He hardly even talked to her.

Whatever small amount of lust she'd thought was there in the beginning, was gone now. Maybe she had been mistaken. Jessenia would do better to keep her head down and learn what she could about her powers and casting as a whole. Then, when she had enough money saved, she could leave the Keep.

Her heart hurt at the thought, but she didn't belong there. She was not a Guardian, and she obviously was not mated to one.

No, she did not belong there.

Chapter Three

"C*ump*, I fucked this all up," Furio snorted. He shook his head from side to side, causing his thick hair to tumble from its confines. He tried to catch his breath, but aside from the physical strain of the work they were doing, he was all torn up inside.

The end of February meant the heart of winter in the Garden State, but that wasn't going to stop either Shifter from getting the job done. Kingston had started the project, but Furio jumped on board from the get-go. It was the least he could do to make amends.

The greenhouse was a surprise for the Alpha's mate, and coincidentally for Jessenia. The cold could suck his dick, for all he cared. He was a mother-fucking Stallion baby. Cold meant shit to him. He would always do what was required of him, regardless of any weather.

Besides, this was something close to his heart. He had been watching for months, storing away tiny fragments of information about the curvy little kitchen Witch as he noticed them. Jessenia was a marvelous chef. She was always running to the market for fresh herbs and things like that.

All for the wonderful concoctions she constantly whipped together for the Guardians. He hated that she had to work so hard to get them, and her disappointment when they were out of something was his own.

Fucking hell. He sounded like a goddamn pussy. His Stallion stomped at the description, and he closed his eyes to rein in the animal. Nah, the beast was right. If it meant something to her, it meant something to him. Even though she'd rebuffed him after the first *and only* time he'd kissed her, Furio was still hooked.

She was his mate. That was how these things worked, he figured. It didn't matter how she acted towards him. Not that she behaved badly, she just wasn't into him. Shit, that sucked to admit, but there it was.

Even though now and then he swore he'd caught a whiff of her arousal, he could bever be sure, fleeting as the scent it was. Anyway, back to the reason he was outside in the freezing cold. His fated mate was a chef and a Witch. She would damn well have fresh herbs at her disposal year-round if he had anything to say about it.

"What are you talking about? You fucked what up? The frame looks straight," the Dragon grunted, and lifted a huge pane of glass to fit into the slot.

"Yeah, the frame is fine," he growled, and held it while the Dragon slid that last piece into the metal frame.

Furio had only just finished securing the hunk of metal to the frozen ground with four feet of rebar and a big fucking sledgehammer. Good thing they had plenty of Shifter strength between the two of them to complete the project.

Sure, they'd already prepped the outdoor kitchen garden for planting in the spring, but that would not be useable for another few months at least. Holley and Jessenia had already used up every free inch of space to sit their potted herbs and plants on in the kitchen, dining, and living rooms. It was getting to the point where they had to stand to eat.

Kingston had finally realized there was no stopping his mate when it came to growing things, so he planned this greenhouse as a Valentine's Day surprise. Unfortunately, rounding up the remaining Loyalists in the area was proving more difficult than they'd imagined, and they were already late with the little project.

"So, what are you talking about then? The gutters?" Kingston asked and wiped his brow.

"I don't mean the greenhouse."

"Ah, you are speaking of our resident kitchen Witch then," the Dragon smirked, and Furio's Stallion whinnied.

The fucker always knew what was going on within the Keep and among his Guardians. Furio supposed it came with his job. He could not have had a more patient and knowledgeable Alpha if he'd gone and searched for one.

And yet, Kingston was so much more than that to him. The Diamond Dragon deserved his respect and unwavering loyalty.

"Yeah," he said honestly, "She still isn't talking to me. Well, not really. Every time I walk into a room, she runs the other way."

"I've noticed things seem tense," Kingston grunted as he tried to delicately drive in the screws holding the last pane in place.

"It all started when I was being an ass to you and Holley," he fessed up, shrugging, and trying like hell to not completely wuss out.

"I see," Kingston returned carefully.

"I can't even tell you how much I regret that, bro."

"I understand, Furio," his Alpha turned to him, "You loved Neela. We all did, in our own ways. I get that you thought I was being disloyal."

"It wasn't my place, *cump*," he clenched his jaw, "I am so sorry about that. Seriously, Holley is wonderful, and she deserved better from me. Neela was a great friend, and no, she didn't deserve to die. Not the way she did," he shook his head emphatically, "But that wasn't your fault. I knew that then, and I know it now. She was great, but she wasn't your fated mate."

"Furio, you don't have to say this," he placed a hand on the other man's shoulder, and the Stallion trembled under the weight of his good Alpha's stare.

"I just, I wanted you to know, I can tell the difference now, between one who is a mate and one who is not. I am so sorry for giving you shit, bro," he closed his eyes, feeling a lighter now that he'd said it all.

"It's all good," Kingston said, "I know you were going through something. Maybe the circumstances with your own parents too, yeah?"

"Yeah," he sniffed, turning his head.

Kingston knew the whole sad fucking story of his past, and Furio didn't want to rehash it. Not here. Not now. Especially not when he could hear footsteps in the snow, and he knew exactly who they belonged to.

Neigh. Stomp. Fuck yeah.

Shit. His Stallion whinnied and stomped inside his mind's eye. The huge Draft Horse had a thick-muscled white body, with a dark ebony mane and tale. Unique among Shifter species, he was the only one left of his kind that he knew of.

Truth was, he did not know what to expect from his Horse. A prey animal, it was odd for a warrior like him to not be a large predator, but instinct wise, he was on the money when it came to fighting. In battle, there was no more reliable a fighter than Furio. He was proud of his rep in that respect.

Of course, he was not so proud of his behavior the last few months. But he would work on regaining some of what he'd lost. Even if it killed him.

His human hair was much the same as his animal side. Long, dark, thick tresses that he kept back from his face with a vegan leather thong. He kept a close-cropped beard year-round, nothing more than scruff really, and he preferred flannel and denim to suits or leather.

Unlike many of the supernaturals in his group of Guardians, Furio was a vegetarian. And like his Italian heritage suggested, he preferred pasta to steak any day of the week. Of course, greens were his chocolate.

It was another reason he'd volunteered to help build the greenhouse. Also, there was the tiny fact he was a trained carpenter. After his parents had died, but before he'd become a Guardian, Furio had spent weekends doing carpentry work.

Papa was a Shifter like him, but his Mama was a *normal*. A wonderful chef and brilliant mother. Damn, he missed them like hell. Could still hear their screams sounding off inside his head when the car his father had been driving had spun out of control.

They'd been on their way home from the shore after a weekend getaway, and the weather had turned bad suddenly. The freak storm was unnatural, a manifestation of Dark Witches, he'd later found out.

Furio had been twelve at the time. Neither of his parents survived the accident. Just him. Afterwards, he went where most destitute male Shifters in the Garden State ended up, St. Christopher's Orphanage.

Not something that was widely advertised, the orphanage used to be run by the Hounds of God. An old Werewolf organization who used to answer to the Catholic Church. As far as he knew, the Wardens of Terra had taken over after the Hounds were disbanded, but the place was still up and running.

And his old principal, Sister Margaret, still worked on keeping little shits like himself in line. Furio sent the older nun and Doe Shifter, a fruit basket and hefty donation every Christmas like clockwork. It was the least he could do, considering she'd saved his life.

"You know, they would be proud of you, Fur," Kingston said, squeezing his shoulder, but the Horse merely grunted.

By the time he'd turned seventeen, Furio was into anything that could help him forget about his past. He'd tried drinking, drugs, wild parties, and even a misdemeanor or two. It wasn't until another boy he was hanging around with almost died after an allergic reaction to some pills they'd scored, that he'd wised up.

He'd gone to Sister Margaret's office, red-eyed from crying, and she had called a number. Twenty-minutes later, a silver car pulled up, and out stepped the most ferocious looking fucker he'd ever seen.

Kingston Baldric. The badass Diamond Dragon was there to whip Furio into shape. And did he? Fuck yeah.

"My name is Kingston," he'd said, *"You about ready to stop fucking around, and be part of some-thing valuable?"*

"Whatcha talkin' 'bout?" an incredibly young and stupid Furio had returned.

"I am talking about bad guys. Real ones. Like the ones who conjured the storm that killed your parents."

"You know who killed Papa and Mama?"

"I know the group claiming responsibility for that thunderstorm. What I want to know, is do you have what it takes to best them?"

"Fuck yeah, cump," he'd growled.

"We'll see, cump," the Dragon spat back.

Sister Margaret had hugged him goodbye, and he still hadn't realized then how much she had helped him. Wouldn't know what she did for him until years later.

Kingston had driven him home to the Keep. He'd been patient with the streetwise kid and helped turn him into a man. Hell, they all had. Each of the Guardians had taught him something. Shit, they taught him *everything* he knew.

He'd met Byram, Egros, Elena and Storm. And of course, Neela too. The she-Dragon was the most beautiful woman he'd ever seen, and she'd smiled at him. She made the Keep feel like a home when the rest were still trying to size him up.

"I am still here, if you need to talk," Kingston said before the door swung open.

Then she was standing there, and he couldn't think, much less speak. Surrounded by big, white snowflakes, some of which landed in her hair, making it glisten and sparkle, Jessenia glided inside. Sharing the same space with her was about as real as shit got. Far as he was concerned, it was heaven.

"Wow! You sure did a lot of work in just a few hours," she studied the room almost as if she could see it filled with plants.

"We're Shifters," Kingston winked at the tiny woman, and Furio's Stallion snorted angrily.

Damn beast was possessive as fuck over his

piccolina. Had been ever since he'd first laid eyes on that messy bun. She always wore her curly chestnut locks that way. They framed her heart-shaped face and made those crazy pink lips even more kissable in his humble opinion.

Mincha! How he wanted her. Furio didn't want to blink. Afraid she'd disappear in the time it took to close and open his eyes again, he stood completely still and stared.

Shit. He was an idiot, but she was perfect. Tempting and beautiful, cheeks pink from the cold, eyes sparkling like amber crystals, and smelling for all the world like the best damn thing he ever scented. And she was all his, even if the sassy female didn't know it.

Mine.

Chapter Four

Jessenia Banks, the gorgeous curvy little kitchen Witch that he nicknamed *piccolina*, was his one true and fated mate. Only, she didn't know it.

Had no clue, in fact. And why didn't she know it? That was actually kinda complicated. His Stallion snorted, and he could feel the animal's criticism down to his bones.

Okay, fine. Maybe it wasn't complicated. Maybe she didn't know a thing about it because he didn't have the fucking balls to tell her.

Shit. Sometimes being a Shifter sucked. He couldn't lie, not even to himself. The acrid stench that came with lies turned his stomach. It just wasn't an option for him.

Still, how could he tell that perfect, beautiful, classy woman that she belonged with him? He was a fucking Neanderthal compared to her. From what he could tell, Jessenia was smart. Like super smart. When she wasn't cooking up a storm, she was producing videos for her website and writing articles. And when she wasn't doing that, she was reading. Like all the time. *For fun.*

Furio was not a big reader. Truth was, he'd been diagnosed with dyslexia after his parent's accident, which explained his bad grades. It was probably also the reason he'd always preferred to work with his hands.

Yeah. He was no good for her. Jessenia was better than him in so many ways. But knowing it still couldn't stop him from wanting her. He'd probably go to his grave wanting the beautiful Witch.

It didn't matter though. She hated his guts. Had basically told him to fuck off ever since he'd acted like an ass to Holley.

There it was. Another strike against him, in his campaign to impress the Witch and make her see what a catch he was.

Snort. As if. Furio wasn't even in the same category. Besides Jessenia's affection for Holley, which was obvious, she seemed completely immune to his charms. She spent all her time with Kingston's mate and her other BFF, Fergie.

He couldn't fault her there. Both women had wormed their way into his heart as well. Storm's mate was feisty and fun to be with. And Holley, well, she was amazing. And she was good for Kingston, which meant the world to him.

He owed the Dragon so much. Especially his loyalty. Furio's initial reaction to his Alpha's claiming Holley as his mate shamed both his human and Stallion sides. But he couldn't turn back time, no matter how much he wanted to.

The past was the past, and though he would never forget Neela or how good she'd been to him, he understood the Dragons' relationship was not what he'd thought. The revelation that Kingston had been honoring Edgar, willingly giving his own freedom to fulfill his fallen brother's dying wish, had been a shock.

Furio could only try to understand that kind of bond. Without a family of his own, it was hard as hell. The Guardians of Chaos were the closest thing he had to family. So, yeah, it had taken him some time, but he now could say he was genuinely happy that his Alpha had found and claimed his fated mate. A state he envied the man.

"Is Holley alright?" Kingston's voice broke through Furio's silent monologue as Jessenia looked around the greenhouse.

"What? Oh, yes, I'm sorry," she smiled, "She's fine, but she wanted me to remind you that her appointment is for three. It's two-thirty now."

"Is it? Shit. Furio, can you finish in here?" Kingston wiped his hands on his jeans and hauled his ass out the door before Furio could do more than nod in response.

"I am on it, bro," he returned, attempting to cover up the awkwardness he felt being alone with her.

"Wow, this is awesome," she spun around in a circle as she took in the empty space.

As far as greenhouses went, it was small, but empty like this, it appeared larger. She was smiling widely, like she couldn't help herself as she walked the length of the room, and he was powerless to do anything but watch.

"It's, uh, kinda small," he said inanely, "Just a simple thirty by fifteen-foot rectangle made of steel and glass."

Simple alright, but with her inside, it was his new favorite place. He swallowed down his nerves and waited for her to respond.

"Well, I think it's great! What's this over here?"

she pointed up, and Furio took the opportunity to wipe his suddenly sweaty palms on the front of his shirt.

"Oh, that's a gutter system. It'll catch rainwater."

"Oh?"

"Yeah, it will repurpose rainwater and melting snow to benefit the plants once this place is filled. We're gonna put in a whole hydroponics garden on this side, with an overflow drainage system to prevent flooding. Some raised plots over there, and a rust-free, wire-shelving system in the back. There's going to be a furnace in the center, to heat the space in winter," he explained, watching greedily for signs of approval.

Fuck, he was like a kid again. Waiting for his teachers to notice when he did something right. He only hoped he didn't lash out and embarrass himself like he used to when praise proved beyond him. But he did not need to worry. He didn't want her praise, not exactly. He just wanted to be with her. Like this.

His Stallion nodded his great equine head in approval. Yes. Being with her was good. A soothing balm for his soul.

"Really? That sounds so amazing," her eyes twinkled in her excitement, "Holley will love it."

"It's not just for Holley," he murmured, the

could've cursed himself when she slowly turned to face him.

"It's not?"

"Nah," he shook his head, "uh, anyone can use it."

"Yeah?"

"Yeah, like, you know, for herbs for cooking maybe, or potions," he shrugged.

Mincha! He sounded like a fucking moron. But what could he say? She was so pretty, he could hardly maintain a coherent thought.

Those big brown eyes were his undoing. Not to mention those soft-looking, wild curls framing her face. His pants were growing tight around his suddenly hard cock, but he could not look way.

Furio wanted to cuddle her close and nuzzle the flesh beneath her ear. To breath in that fresh, earthy *basilico* scent that clung to her.

He loved basil. It was his favorite herb. That she should smell like that one thing above all others made his Stallion whinny and stomp like a racehorse about to bolt right out of the gate.

Fuck, he would run a thousand miles just to get a whiff of her. And that thought alone kept his hands firmly stuck in his pockets. Furio knew if he even came close to her, all bets were off. The fragile truce that existed between them was too precious to break.

The hold he had on the metaphorical reins that held his Stallion back was precarious at best. He heard the smile in her voice as she asked intelligent questions about the design, and he basked in it. Furio was only too happy to stay with her, to explain anything she wanted to know about the construct of the small building.

"How do you know so much about all this?" she asked.

"What? Construction?"

"Yeah," she shrugged.

He felt his cheeks heat up as he rushed to think of an explanation. Fuck it. Might as well go with the truth.

"It was one of the things I learned back at St. Christopher's," he sucked in a breath.

Shit. He hadn't meant to let that slip out first.

"St. Chrisopher's over in Montville?"

Her eyes widened, and he turned around roughly. The last thing he wanted was her pity. Why the fuck had he ever said that? He could have kicked himself, but his animal snorted.

The beast reminded him he had nothing to be ashamed of. His past couldn't be helped, but his future could. And if he were lucky, she would be in it.

"I think that's great," she continued.

"What? That I grew up in an orphanage?"

He was being a dick. He knew it, but he couldn't help it. Shit. It was the last thing he wanted. Seemed whenever he was around the woman, Furio couldn't help but make an ass of himself.

"Furio, I didn't mean to trivialize or poke fun at you. I don't know what you went through. I don't really know anything about you but-"

"No, you don't know," he gritted his teeth, "but whatever, right? Not all of us have perfect lives. We can't all have loads of friends, family, that kind of shit, right? Whatever."

The feel of Jessenia's small hand on his arm brought his head whipping around to the side. When did she walk across the room? Shit. He was really out of it if this little female could sneak up on him.

"Hey, I didn't mean it like that, Furio," she said his name with a slight accent that made his heart thud steadily inside his chest, "You know, I didn't have a perfect family either. My parents, well my mother, had denied her heritage for a long time. When I found out I had magic, it was a complete shock. She and my dad hated that I wanted to embrace my powers."

"What?" he asked, not bothering to hide his surprise.

His Stallion snorted. Right then, he wanted to find her parents and knock their heads together. How could anyone not be thrilled to have this gifted, beautiful Witch in their lives?

"Yeah, we still don't talk much. I mean," she shrugged a little self-consciously.

Furio sucked in a breath. He had to make fists with his hands to stop from reaching out to touch her. It wasn't his place. He'd tried that once, and she'd refused him. Maybe she just didn't like him. What the fuck did he know?

Now and then he thought he saw a spark of interest, but it was always fleeting. Wishful thinking, he guessed. Either way, she was talking now, and he wanted to hear more. So he nodded, encouraging her to go on.

"I learned about cooking and healing potions from my grandmother. My parents were horrified. Eventually, I went to live with her. They were just not that interested in me once I embraced my supernatural heritage. Granny was exceptional, but she was older. I was lonely."

"Shit, Jess," he got the words out barely above a whisper.

"Don't be. I pretty much gave up on them by the time I reached high school, and I guess I haven't spoken to them in years. Fergie was my only friend after that."

"I'm sorry," he frowned down at her, and he meant it.

No one should treat her that way. She was a gift. A fucking treasure. She deserved so much better.

We can give her everything she needs. Be her family. Her home. His Stallion pushed the thoughts at him, but he ignored the beast. Jessenia deserved better than him.

"Anyway," she swallowed.

"My mother and father died in a car crash. It's how I wound up at St. Christopher's," he confessed his past to her like it was some sin he carried.

He knew better. He really did, but deep down, he'd always felt as if he were being judged whenever people discovered the truth about his family. He'd had distant cousins, but no one who was willing to take on a tough as nails teen with a chip on his shoulder.

"Oh, Furio, I am so sorry," Jessenia stepped forward and impulsively gave him a hug.

The hard, brief contact set his entire body aflame, and it was all he could do not to return the embrace tenfold. As it was, she'd let go before he could even react.

"This really looks good. I think it's going to be great," she said, her brown eyes taking in the place once more, and he could see her excitement.

Hell, it was all over her now. Radiating off of her curvy little form in waves that seemed to wrap around him, making his Stallion whinny and his cock hard. He licked his lips and moved closer, crowding her.

She didn't flinch when he invaded her space, in fact, she seemed to lean into him. As if seeking his heat. Maybe she was. It was fifteen degrees outside, and the wind was whipping against the glass panes of the greenhouse.

"I should get back," her voice was low, but he had excellent hearing.

"Yeah," he agreed, "you should."

But still, his hands came up to grip her waist. Furio tugged her towards him until her lush body was flush against his hard one. If not for that hug she'd given him, he would never have dared such a bold move.

It was too late to close the floodgates now. Need

pulsed through him, and he took in a deep breath. Sucking air greedily into his lungs, swallowing down Jessenia's fresh basil scent. It tickled his senses, teased him with promises of passion and joy, and before he could stop himself, he lowered his head.

"Furio," she whispered his name, but she was pulling him closer too.

The action meant something. It just had to, right? He felt the growl build up inside his chest, and his lips came crashing down onto hers.

Holding on to his self-control by a thread, Furio claimed Jessenia's mouth with all the pent-up passion he'd been saving for her for months now. The world seemed to tilt on its axis, and fuck if he didn't hear the tide turn from all the way out there, deep in the Pine Barrens.

Kissing Jessenia was addictive, and yet it wasn't what he'd been meaning to do. Their shared kiss was not the soft, fairytale whisper he'd wanted to give her. It wasn't patient, or calm, or kind. No, it was like him, rough around the edges, demanding, and a little unrestrained.

They collided like two opposing forces, and the result was a phenomenon unlike any other. Like light and dark, refined and raw, soft and hard. She was his perfect counterpart. As if she'd been waiting for this moment too, she sighed and melted into him.

Jessenia's throat vibrated with her moan as she accepted his kiss, and even more astounding, kissed him back. Furio's body hummed with anticipation and barely restrained power as he continued to test and tease her silken lips.

Encouraged by the not so small fact she hadn't slapped his face, he pushed his tongue inside the hot cavern of her mouth. Testing, tasting, pushing his advantage until he felt the tiny pricks of her nails digging into the flesh of his shoulders. But still, she was not pushing him away. That fact had his blood singing in his veins. If anything, his *piccolina* was dragging him even closer.

"Come here," he growled, lifting her up until she wrapped her legs around his waist.

He held on to her, cupping the round globes of her perfect peach of an ass as he plundered her mouth. She tasted better than he could've ever imagined. Like sunshine and sin. A dangerous mix for sure. One he was sure to crave again and again.

"Mine," the word slipped from his lips as she slowed the kiss.

Big brown eyes bore into his, and Jessenia suddenly pushed against his hold. Reluctantly, he let her go. But he was helpless to stop the shiver that went through him as she slid down his body until her booted feet hit the floor.

"I, uh, I should get back," she was a little unsteady on her feet, but declined his outstretched hand.

That hurt a lot admittedly, but Furio remained still. He might not understand everything that just happened, but he instinctively knew she needed space. In fact, it was a great idea.

Watching from the doorway until she was safely tucked away inside the Keep, he turned and paced up and down until he stood at the back of the greenhouse. She'd been so excited about it. He was determined to stay up all night if he had to, just to finish the damn thing. But first things first, he thought with a sigh.

Furio stripped off his clothing and stepped outside. The sun had set, but that happened early this time of year, and it couldn't have been later than three or four. Fuck it, he thought and began to run, transforming into his Stallion mid-stride.

It was not something every Shifter could accomplish, but it was one trick he'd learned early on. Storm always said it must be a trait unique to Horse Shifters, but he wasn't sure the Wolf wasn't simply jealous. That would be funny, he thought. There was no need for envy among them. Each Guardian had their own talents and specialties.

In fact, he'd never begrudged any of the members of his group their abilities. The only time he felt that green-eyed monster, and he didn't mean himself, was when he watched Storm or Kingston with their mates. Egros, Byram and Elena didn't get it. He'd met his mate, and the fact he didn't have her was driving him mad.

The kiss had been promising, but something shifted just at the end. Fuck all if he knew what had happened. One thing he understood was Furio needed this. To run, to stretch his long legs, and work out the pent-up passion bubbling inside of him.

True, he'd rather do that between the sheets with his mate, but she needed time and space. It might kill him, but he would give it to her.

Neigh. His Stallion whinnied furiously at the thought. Death was not an option. Not when he had a mate to claim, protect, and cherish. And he would. Just as soon as he figured out how to convince her to take him on.

Mine.

Chapter Five

"Wait," Fergie stalked after Jessenia with her mouth full of gooey chocolate from the fresh baked muffin she'd taken out of the oven minutes ago.

She'd been up all night long, tossing and turning. Ever since she'd kissed that long-haired pain in her ass. What the hell was that, anyway?

He'd picked her up like she weighed nothing and took her mouth as if he'd owned it. Then he'd said something. One word which had sent her straight to the library for some research.

Mine. He'd said *mine.* She scoured the ancient reference books documenting Shifter behavior in the old Keep's amazing library, and the result was disturbing. Not unwelcomed per se, but it shook her to her core.

"Jess," Fergie interrupted her train of thought as she busied herself cleaning bowls and loading the dishwasher, "You guys kissed? For real?"

Her BFF squeaked loudly, and Jessenia covered her ears. Dang Wolf Shifter vocal cords. They were going to be the death of her.

"Shhh! Do you want everyone to hear you?" she grumbled.

"Sorry," Fergie giggled, straightening her dark purple blouse as she did so, "Besides, it ain't like it's a big secret. You and *Mr. Fast and Furio-us* have not been exactly unnoticeable. And I see you made carrot cake again."

"For real?" she asked, ignoring the carrot cake remark.

Okay. So, she knew he liked it. He wasn't the only one, right? Shit. She picked up the cake and tossed it in the trash.

"Hey! What gives?"

"Nothing. Just answer the question."

"Fine. Yeah, for real you guys might as well be wearing a sign! *Sheesh.* But anyway, did you, see what I did there? *Mr. Fast and Furio-us?*" she snorted.

"Yes, Fergie, very clever," Jessenia rolled her eyes, "But what do you mean we aren't unnoticeable?"

"Girl, those big brown puppy eyes of yours follow him around like all the dang time."

"What? *Nuh uh.*"

"Yeah huh," Fergie said, confirming Jessenia's worst fears.

Great. So, it turned out her whole *if-I-ignore-these-feelings-they-will-go-away* plan didn't not only fail, but everyone, including the object of her affection, was in on it.

WTF. Was the whole world out to get her? Or just the supernatural one? Ugh.

"Why didn't you tell me it was obvious?" she demanded and cursed under her breath.

"Because Jess, you know how you are," Fergie said.

"What the heck kind of an answer is that? How am I?"

"Well, for one thing, you and a certain *Italian Stallion* have got like so much sexual tension between you, I'm surprised you can even see two feet in front of you."

"OMG! No, you did not just say that? Like, do

you mean he knows? He's like known this whole time?"

This time, Jessenia was the one who squeaked. Dropping her head into her arms, she leaned on the island in the middle of the kitchen. Crap. How was she going to face him?

"Hey," Fergie leaned closer, but Jessenia was too shocked to answer.

Was it that obvious? Did everyone know she had the hots for the Stallion? OMG. Did Fergie just call him the *Italian Stallion?* That was it.

Jessenia was going to kill Fergie, but it would have to wait. Her shoe inclined friend was still going strong. Her brows furrowed as she waited to hear what the redhead was going to blurt next.

"Between us besties, is he really, you know, *hung like a horse?*" Fergie reached out to snag another muffin, but Jessenia had reached the end of her rope.

Even best friends had boundaries, and Fergie had just crossed hers. Enough was enough. Jessenia straightened and picked up the wooden spoon she'd used to mix the batter, then she whacked Fergie right on her ass with the thing.

"Ow! Oh my God! Jess, how could you?" she hissed, "There was still batter on that, and now my pants are dirty."

"Boo hoo! The Keep will wash them. Now, what else do you know about all this between me and Furio? I spent all night trying to find out anything, but those old books need to update their indexes," she stomped her foot on the tiled floor. Not very effective considering she wore her favorite lime green Crocs at the moment.

"Ouch. My butt still hurts," Fergie whined.

"Serves you right," Jessenia pursed her lips, "Now, no more penis references before coffee, and I said those were for *later*. Now, tell me what you meant about knowing how things were between me and Furio?"

"Jess, I didn't mean anything," Fergie pouted, but she was so not getting another muffin until she explained herself, "I just meant you always do this when you like a guy. You get down on yourself and start acting like you aren't good enough for him. I don't want to see you go through that again. Besides, he's a Shifter."

"What? I do not, and so what, your guy is a Shifter," Jessenia frowned.

She started plucking still warm muffins from their pans and stacking the chocolate chip and banana nut goodies into two separate baskets with a little more vigor than anticipated. The result was one or two muffin casualties. *Sigh.*

"Actually, you do, Jess," Fergie insisted gently, "but if what you said about your kiss is true," she grinned widely, "I think this time you don't have to worry about all that."

"What are you talking about?"

"He said 'mine' right? When he kissed you?" Fergie asked.

"So?" Jessenia had thought the whole monosyllabic word was weird at the end of their kiss, but the truth was, she was kind of into it.

The whole growly, possessive thing he had going on during their heated exchange made her panties soaked with desire. In fact, the whole thing had filled her with torturous anticipation. She'd half expected him to hunt her down in her bedroom that night.

Okay, so it was more like she'd wished for that. Waking up extra early the next morning under the guise of baking fresh muffins had not resulted in catching a glimpse of the handsome Stallion. Much to her dismay.

"Well," Fergie said while she poured a second cup of fresh brewed Columbian roast, "Shifters only say that when they meet their mates."

The sound of the muffin tin hitting the tiled floor

rang throughout the room like a bullet being fired from close range.

"Excuse me?" Jessenia's heart began to pound, and that bubbly, zippy little feeling that was her usual magic went a little bit haywire inside of her.

"I said, it means you're probably his mate," Fergie's eyes went wide, and she heard her friend's hesitation.

"And how long does it take for a Shifter to realize someone is his or her mate?" she asked far too casually.

"Uh, immediately?" Fergie winced.

"I see," Jessenia said between gritted teeth.

She turned around and picked up the tin form the floor. Stacking the empty bakeware in a pile, she hardly registered the sounds of footsteps running towards them.

In fact, it was a full minute before she stopped what she was doing and looked to see three pairs of curious eyes on her. One bright green pair seemed a little tense. Maybe agitated was a better way to describe them. To her, those eyes were of particular interest.

"Mates? We're mates? And you didn't think to tell me?"

"Uh-" Furio opened and closed his mouth a few times, but Jessenia was so not having that.

He was wearing a pair of sweats and a tank top, typical sparing gear. Similar to what the other two Guardians had on. They must have started in the training room early that morning. Too early for her to have caught them when she started baking.

"Well, Furio? Is that true?"

"Jessenia, I, I mean," he swallowed then narrowed his eyes at her and the other people in the room seemed to fade away, "Yes. You're my mate."

"When?" she asked, "When did you know?"

"Um, I think we should go now," Fergie grabbed Storm's arm, tugging her mate out of the line of fire. *Smart,* she thought with a frown as she squared off in front of *him.* Anger and confusion warred within her. Was there something wrong with her? Did he think she wasn't good enough for him?

"Jessenia, we should talk," he said.

"When did you know?" she repeated.

"Everything okay here? Good, I am going to just go back to my room," Elena's pink gaze flashed between the angry kitchen Witch, and the confused Stallion.

Jessenia felt her anger rise. When that happened, her powers tended to go wonky, but she did not give a shit. A dozen nameless emotions batted up against the shield she'd constructed around her heart long ago to protect herself, the foremost of which was hurt.

Why hadn't he told her? Was he ashamed? She was only a kitchen Witch. She was not clever like Fergie, nor was she a powerful practitioner like Holley. The Guardians' mates were kickass, but maybe she didn't measure up.

"Let me explain," he tried to reason, but she was not in the mood.

"Were you ever going to tell me?"

"Jessenia," he called her name in a plaintive, husky whisper that went straight to her core.

But she ignored her body's cry for attention. She was too angry for that. Hell, she was pissed off, and rightly so.

"How long have you known?"

"That you're my mate?" he asked, and she wanted to whack him over the head with the wooden spoon that was still in her hand.

"Yes," she growled between gritted teeth, "How long?"

"Since the first time I saw you," he finally confessed, and the world seemed to go still.

Silence. Deafening silence pounded against her.

Then, it was a roaring tidal wave. No longer a still rock, her whole world was hurtling through space and time breaking records and barriers like an out-of-control asteroid.

Fucking hell. She needed a grip. Her magic sizzled and sparked. Angry as she was, it was a miracle she didn't burn the place down. But she was just a little kitchen Witch. Not dangerous, not important, and apparently not mate material.

"Well, isn't this great!"

Okay. Jessenia was full on screaming now. She paced back and forth along the tiled floor to try and regain her composure, but it was too much. All her life she'd been made to feel as if she were not good enough by the people who should have treasured her the most.

Her own parents denied her existence. She was nothing but a disappointment to them. A thorn in their sides. She knew Witches did not always have mates. But the truth was, after Fergie, *a normal*, had met her own fated mate, Jessenia wished for one of her own.

Someone who would truly want her. As is, no returns or exchanges. A mate of her very own to treasure and love. Someone to talk to and experience life with. A real friend. A soulmate. That was her secret dream, and she'd never been more ashamed of it than right now.

Ever since she'd met the Guardians, *Furio in particular*, Jessenia had to admit a certain affinity for the Stallion.

Fine. She'd been hot and bothered since she'd laid eyes on him. With his long chestnut hair, dark green eyes, straight nose, and impossibly gorgeous body, how was she supposed to resist?

She'd managed to keep her distance, barely. Downplaying her attraction and hiding her response to him for months now. But then yesterday after-noon, he'd kissed her. And like a complete idiot, she'd started to hope that maybe something could develop between them. Something more.

She had no idea his fervently whispered "mine" was a confession of sorts. When she'd confided in Fergie, she was hoping to glean some knowledge about how starting a relationship with a Shifter.

Her bestie had an in with Shifters that even as a supernatural Jessenia had not been privy too. She had no idea his gravelly voice was anything more than simply sexy when he'd uttered *mine* after they'd kissed.

Okay, so maybe she'd hoped it meant what it meant. But and this was a big fat horse's ass of a *but*, she'd been unaware that Shifters could tell their mates at first sniff. Once confirmed, it was something she could not un-know.

"So, what? You figured I wasn't good enough for you, so you just ignored it? You ignored me?"

"Jessenia, please listen. I swear, that is not why I didn't tell you," he stepped towards her, but she was still raw.

Her power jumped out at him, stopping him mid-stride. She was breathing heavily. Anger seeped from her pores.

"I don't believe you," she hissed, and her magic flared.

She could see him straining against it, trying to move towards her. Crap. She didn't know what was happening. Had never had her magic react like that.

She was just a kitchen Witch. Nothing to write home about. Her magic allowed her to create healing salves and potions from common ingredients found in the average kitchen and some not so common herbs and things. That was all.

And no, she did not use eye of newt, fuck you very much. Those kinds of stereotypes really pissed her off. As did lies of any kind, even omission. Still, her magic was not offensive, meaning it was not actively aggressive or used for fighting. But maybe she would have to change her mind about that, she thought as her powers lashed out with her hurt.

Jessenia could not believe she'd spent weeks, no, make that months, secretly pining for the long-haired jerk! She was his mate, for fuck's sake! His mate, only he did not want her. Humiliation threatened to send her to her knees, but she held on to her anger instead.

Of course, that led to her powers zapping him again, which was not this kitchen Witch's intention at all. She was a healer. Only right then, she didn't feel like helping. Like, not at all.

"Ow! Fuck. Please, Jessenia," he begged.

Furio was sucking in air rapidly, but her magic continued to bind him. Anger and hurt made her blind to his pain. She felt like a total idiot. How could she be so stupid? She was a fool for believing in that kiss! She'd built castles on one insignificant meeting of lips.

Only a sad and desperate woman would do such a thing. She gritted her teeth as those words filled her brain. She'd wanted happily ever after. Instead, she got a reluctant mate. Hell! Of course, love would not be easy for her.

It never was.

Chapter Six

Anger and humiliation, along with a healthy dose of contempt, self and otherwise, made Jessenia feel like a powder keg ready to blow.

She'd been fighting her attraction to him to save her pride, and the very moment she'd let her guard down, things went to shit.

"I made a mistake," he grunted.

"Why? Why did you lie to me?"

"No lie," he tried to respond.

But she was too angry to hear him. Furio had known the entire time what she was to him. He knew from the moment he'd met her in that coffee shop when she'd been worried about Fergie's safety that she was his mate. He just didn't want her.

When Storm had turned out to be Fergie's fated mate, Jessenia had been in awe of their connection. Immediate, instantaneous, powerful, and mutual. There was nothing like it in the entire universe.

So yeah, she was happy for her friend, and a little envious. Okay. A lot envious. How could she not be? Having a fated mate was like getting a gift from the universe itself.

Your very own guaranteed-to-love-you-warts-and-all significant other to be yours for all time. Who didn't want one of those?

Shit. Her hurt was tangible now, and her magic was acting as an extension of that pain and anguish. No, she didn't want to hear anymore.

"Give me a second," he gasped, but she was not listening.

She couldn't. Not when tears threatened to spill any moment.

"Have to explain," Furio struggled against the invisible ropes of her power that held him hostage.

No matter how hard he tried, he couldn't break them. That fact salvaged whatever pride she had left. Or it would have. But then she took a good look at him.

"Oh my God!" Fergie came running towards her,

but her magic had created some sort of barrier between the kitchen and the rest of the Keep.

"Jessenia! You have to stop," she yelled, but Jessenia was not paying any attention to her former roommate.

Her eyes were on Furio, and they widened in horror as his face turned a terrible shade of red. She was doing that to him. The realization froze her.

Her magic was making it impossible for him to move. No, it was making it impossible for the man *to breathe*. She whimpered, and clapped a hand over her mouth.

"Oh shit," she closed her eyes, trying to pull back her wayward powers.

Utter horror at what she'd almost done damn near paralyzed her, but she forced herself to focus. It took a moment, but she finally got herself under control. Stunned at what she'd almost done, she sank to the floor and placed both palms on the cold tile.

Jessenia's magic had always ever been a benevolent force. Well, except for that one time, but that was not her fault. She was too young to understand what she was doing. Besides, her mother had ignored that part of her heritage, so she'd had virtually no control of her magic.

That was about the time she'd started lessons

with her grandmother. Even so, a kitchen Witch should not be able to do what she'd almost done. Her mind raced with possible scenarios and what-ifs. Sweat beaded on her brow, and her mouth went dry.

Heart pounding, she could hardly face herself, never mind him. She'd almost killed him! Remorse threatened to choke her as her eyes burned with tears. She would never want to hurt anyone, much less the object of her affections.

Not really, anyway. He might've deserved a thwack on the head, but he definitely didn't deserve to be suffocated by her magic. What the heck was happening to her?

Her body trembled in response to the adrenaline, and her eyes flashed to where Furio fell to his knees gasping for air. Her heart squeezed and she felt sick to her stomach. Magic was not supposed to be used to harm. It went against everything she'd ever believed in.

She turned to stand, needed to leave, to run from the room, but something stopped her. Looking down, she saw his hand wrapped around her ankle. Even though he still struggled for breath, Furio kept a firm hold.

Shit. She couldn't exactly kick him off and run away, now could she? Seconds away from a full-on panic attack, she tried to gently step out of his hold, but the Stallion was too strong.

Oh fuck. What did I almost do?

Embarrassment rose inside her like a vicious bitch of a wind. The kind she saw every February and March in the Garden State. She hated the way it stung her face and made her eyes tear. Only now, it was more like her own outburst that was causing her to want to howl and cry like a banshee.

How could she be so emotional over a guy she kissed once? Just once. But she was, and that was that. Shame and unease caused her to tremble and shake.

He meant so much more to her than *just a guy*. Witches could not always tell their mates the way Shifters could, but she'd recognized Furio from the start. Deep down inside, her soul had kindled in appreciation of his every time she'd looked into his forest-colored eyes.

When he was angry or excited, they glittered like emeralds. But now as he sought to regain his composure, they were dark and cold like the pine trees standing alone, out there in the snow-covered woods.

Shit. She'd really messed up. Even Shifters were under no obligation to claim their mates. What was a mate, really? Just some person, a stranger really. Someone the Fates randomly decided on.

In fact, it was pretty messed up now that she thought about it. Imagine not having a choice about whom to love? Who to be with? Imagine not having any control over your own physical reaction to that person? Maybe she was wrong to be envious of what Fergie had.

At the very least, she'd overreacted. It wasn't even Furio's fault she was caught up in this. If anything, he tried to spare her by not telling her she was his mate.

"I, I have to go," she pulled against his hold, but the Stallion's grip was strong.

"No," he said in his rough-sounding voice, "You got it wrong, *piccolina*. I swear to you."

"No, I was wrong. I was stupid," she sniffed loudly, "I, uh, don't blame you for not wanting me. And I know I sound like an idiot and I acted like a bad person, but I'm not, I swear I didn't mean to hurt you. But, uh, I don't feel sorry for myself either. Not really. I mean, it's not fair to you. Shifters can't pick and choose like the rest of us can, I guess. Look, just let me go-"

"No!" he said roughly, squeezing her ankle

between his long fingers, "I ain't lyin' to you. Never that. I was stupid. Me. Not you. Never you."

"You don't have to say that-"

"Jessenia, just promise you will listen, okay?" he cleared his throat, waiting for her nod, "I'm gonna let go. Promise not to bolt?"

"Yes," Jessenia replied, frozen to the spot.

She couldn't have moved even if she wanted to. Not with him still touching her. As Furio pulled himself up off the ground, his hand never left her. It inched up her leg to her hip, her waist, and finally, her face.

"You got it so wrong, *piccolina*," he grunted, "I want you all right. Let me show you how much," his big hands captured her face, and he pulled her closer.

Eyes wide, she had no time to do anything but react to his blatant display. Raw masculine power exuded from him, unlike anything she'd ever seen.

He was always the joker, the carefree one. Or he had been until Kingston mated Holley. Furio's response to the news that the Witch was his Alpha's fated mate had been less than what she'd expected of him.

But still, she understood it was hurt that drove his actions. Hell, she'd wanted to be the one to soothe him, but all she could do was watch as his harsh words put a wedge between himself and the other Guardians.

She'd seen it all and sympathized with him. But ultimately, she was happy for the Diamond Dragon and for Holley. Overcoming a variety of obstacles, they'd both faced trials during their long lifetimes, and then finding one another was a miracle. Incredible and totally awesome, to be honest. Jessenia was in awe of them both individually and as a mated pair.

The love between them was evident in every passing glance and seemingly casual touch. Kingston's hardened exterior shell had begun to crack and thaw with his mate's careful attentions.

Furio had none of the hostility and anger that so many of his brethren carried within themselves. Or, he hadn't when she'd first met him. He'd been the easygoing one, the clown, but not for months now.

This show of dominance was so unlike the Furio she knew, but it struck a chord within her. Like some ultra-secret feminine part of, buried deep down inside, under all the women's lib beliefs she held dear to her heart, was suddenly stoked to life.

Her skin grew warm as she melted into his taller, wider frame. Furio growled against her lips, wrapping his arms tightly around her body. His soft mouth brushed over hers once, then twice. Insistent, yet tender in his exploration. He licked the seam of her lips, pushing his tongue inside. Searching for more, tasting her very essence, and Jessenia was a goner.

No one had ever kissed her quite like that. It was like the man had a personalized map to her heart and knew exactly how to get there. Well, he knew how to kiss at any rate. Like her every own dream come true.

Towering over her like a pinnacle of physical perfection, Furio kissed, *and kissed,* and kissed her some more. Jessenia was powerless to do anything except react. She heard the others in the periphery, moving away to give the privacy, but she didn't care.

All she wanted was for this kiss to never end. Jessenia ran her hands over his shoulders and down his back, moaning softly as she returned his passion with everything she had.

Hidden desires, secret longings, whispers only lovers would share, all of it and more came rushing forward as their tongues tangled and hearts thudded against each other. He was gorgeous. All long limbs and wiry muscles, demonstrating his speed and strength.

She loved the way he felt pressed against her. All hard and hot, like her own personal furnace.

He smelled incredible, too. Fresh air and cool streams, like the perfect spring day. The kind she longed for, especially now in the dead of winter. New Jersey was notorious for freezing temperatures and endless snows of February as it gave way to March.

But *he* made her feel warm everywhere. He was the promised sunshine of warm days to come, and she longed to bask in his rays. And she would. As long as he never stopped kissing her.

Sigh. His lips warmed hers, caressing the plump mounds until she was limbless. Using him for strength, she moaned as he slowed his silent exploration. Nibbling on her lower lip, his nose brushed against her cheek, and he pressed his forehead gently to hers. Jessenia had to work to slow her breathing, but it was impossible.

Or so it seemed. She wanted him so damn bad. Her sex throbbed, nipples ached, and heart squeezed. And yet, she couldn't help but feel slightly betrayed. She was his mate, and he'd known it all along. Why had he waited so long?

"Jessenia," he whispered her name.

She closed her eyes against the wave of emotion that threatened to send her to her knees. How could she still feel like this?

"That was, uh, nice," she cleared her throat and forced herself out of his embrace.

She almost half-hoped he'd refuse to let go, but he dropped his hands, and allowed her the space she felt she needed. It hurt, she wasn't going to lie to herself.

"Nice? That was more than nice," he frowned.

"Furio," she said his name, savoring it on her lips before pushing the rest of her thoughts through her lips, "you must have had a reason for not wanting to claim me. I guess I will never understand it, but I respect it. Truth is, I don't want to be with someone who has to work himself up to wanting me."

"But that's not it at all. Jessenia? Jessenia!"

He called her name, but she was already walking down the hall to the small bedroom she'd claimed as her own.

She'd stay in there all day if she had to, if only to avoid him. Maybe it was time to move on, she thought and fought against the hurt that rose inside.

This was always supposed to be temporary, she told herself and wiped the tears as she dug out her laptop and began to scroll for a rental.

Chapter Seven

"Well, what did you expect?" Storm slapped Furio in the back of the head.

Normally, he'd have tackled the shit out of the Wolf, but he didn't even have the strength to hit the fucker back. She'd walked away from him. Called him on his bullshit and walked away.

Yeah, he'd fucked this up. And it looked like there was no going back.

"Fuck man, it hurts," the Stallion rubbed the spot on his chest right over his heart.

The muscle was trying to kill him, or at least that was how it felt, how he felt. Strangled and suffocating at the same time. He tried to breathe, but his lungs refused to expand. Damn it, she refused him. Walked away from him.

Shit, shit, shit!

Rejection sucked in general, but being rejected by his fated mate? That was a whole new level of hurt. How did that even happen? He thought mates were supposed to fall in love and live happily ever after, like all the storybooks said.

Well, obviously Furio had been somewhat misinformed. Though, he knew beyond reasonable doubt, he was the cause of all this fuckery. He'd been an asshole for waiting to tell her. Stupid self-doubt. It ate at him, and now his *piccolina* had the short end of the stick.

"It can't be too late, *cump*," Storm shrugged.

"Fuck man, I don't know. Kingston? What about you?" he implored his Alpha.

"Look," the older Dragon said, "the women are all together in Jessenia's bedroom now. I am sure you are the topic of discussion."

"Yeah man, I gotta tell you, from Fergie's texts, it ain't looking good for you," Storm added.

"Fuck," Furio slumped forward, holding his head in his hands.

"Look, Furio, you've always had a difficult time expressing yourself," Kingston addressed him, and his tone held none of the Alpha powers Furio knew were at his fingertips.

This was just a couple of men talking, and for that, he was grateful. Besides, he needed all the advice he could get.

"For a Stallion Shifter, I always thought you were very firmly grounded," Byram said, "None of that aloofness your brethren seem to have inherited, and I liked that about you Furio, I always have," his cool voice only served to confuse him all the more.

"Brethren? You know others like me?"

"Well, not Italian Draft Horses, per se, but I am aware of other Equine Shifters. Jed Thorntree is one. He lives in a little town called Valentine. That's in Texas," the Vampire added, and his Stallion was piqued though now was not really the time.

"So, about Jessenia? How do I get her to forgive me?" he asked, feeling for all the world like the biggest idiot.

"So, what Byram here means, is you should have no problem expressing yourself to your mate," Egros, the only male Witch in the entire Keep piped in.

"Yeah, but you Witches don't have mates like we do," he gestured between himself and the other Shifters in the room, "You don't understand the call."

"Look, Witches may not be able to identify our

fated mates by scent like you all do, but we are super-naturals too. We have fated mates, they are just revealed to us in different ways. Jessenia is a kitchen Witch, so her powers work differently from mine, anyway."

"What's that mean, bro? You tryin' to say my mate isn't powerful?" he growled on the offensive.

"No, man, not at all," Egos raised his hands up to ward off the attack Furio was dying to hurl his way.

Dammit. Now he was losing his shit for no reason at all. The guys were just trying to help him.

"Furio, that's exactly what we are trying to say. That rage is the beast inside of you. He wants his mate," Kingston grinned, obviously enjoying the man's discomfiture, "He's pushing you to claim her, yes?"

"Yes," Furio barely got the word out between gritted teeth.

"I see," he shrugged, "Well, first, you need to woo her."

"I need to *what* her?"

"Not what," Byram grinned along with Kingston "*woo*."

"And how the fuck do I *woo* her? I don't even know what that is, bro," Furio stood up, and paced.

This was so not helping. He was not some

ancient Dragon or suave Vampire. He didn't know shit about fuck when it came to wooing women.

When he'd had an itch in the past, all he really had to do was point and the females would line up to fill his bed.

It wasn't conceit, merely fact. Especially where human women were concerned. Shifters were simply attractive to them. So yeah, he never had to work for sex before. But this, this wasn't sex. This was his mate.

He didn't want to fuck her. Okay, yeah, he did want to fuck her. But it wasn't just fucking. It was something else. A deep-seated, primal instinct that was making his Stallion wild with need.

She was his *fated mate,* or she would be. If he could just get her to listen.

"Look, *cump,* you know I got you, right?" Storm placed his hands on Furio's shoulders, "I wouldn't steer you wrong. What you need to do is flatter her, buy her things, take her places. I recommend shoes-"

"No! Not everyone has a shoe fetish, Storm," Kingston shook his head, "But ice cream can be a good way to bond," he said fondly.

"It's four degrees out," Egros pointed out.

"What about music or a movie?"

"We ain't in high school," he growled in frustration, "No, she deserved something else. Something, special."

"Then I guess, you already know what to do," Kingston nodded.

"Yeah," he said, and walked out of his Alpha's crowded office.

"Hey, Keep," he addressed the home where the Guardians had dwelled for decades, "I know you're listening, and I need your help."

The Keep had a habit of providing for the Guardians on what seemed to be an as-needed basis. Well, Furio sure as fuck needed help right then. He just hoped the Keep would provide.

Working on the greenhouse with Kingston and seeing Jessenia's reaction to it had given him an inkling of what his sassy little kitchen Witch might like. Maybe if he could break through that protective wall he'd helped erect around her heart, he could convince her he was sorry.

Plan in place, he set off towards his suite of rooms on the western side of the manse. The old building was more like a castle in a fairy tale than anything he'd ever seen growing up. Some days, he still couldn't believe he was there at all.

Him. Furio Do Luca, an orphan without a penny to his name, was a Guardian of Chaos. The elite group of supernaturals were renowned for their self-less dedication to the preservation of the freedom of magic for the entire paranormal world.

He'd been assigned to Kingston's group some three decades ago, but he was a Shifter and a Guardian. He did not age the same way normals did, and it showed in his unlined face and still dark hair. But he was still the youngest of their group. Having left the care of St, Christopher's for the Keep at seventeen years old, this was the only home he'd ever known outside of school.

Kingston had been a father-figure of sorts, a friend for sure, and as good an Alpha as he could have ever hoped for. Stallion Shifters were not commonplace, especially in New Jersey, but he was at home in the pine barrens and swamps of the Garden State.

Restless and antsy, his animal had been in a constant state of awareness ever since she'd walked into his life. Jessenia deserved a far better mate than him. But she was his, and he would prove himself worthy. It was all he could do. Fuck that. It was what he had to do, or he might as well just lay down and die. And he was not ready to do that. Die for her, yes. But give up? Fuck no.

"Ah," he grinned, clapping his hands as the door

to his room opened before him, "I can make this will work."

The spirits that dwelled deep within the manse were called the *manetuwak* by Holley, but he would probably just continue to refer to the collective as *the Keep*. It simplified things.

Most of the time he would rather be outside burning off steam with a good, hard run, but this project was special. He'd never had a real home, but he wanted one now. *With her.*

He knew he'd messed up big time, and he had a lot to prove. He wasn't like the others. Not debonair or whatever the fuck, but he was just right for his little *piccolina*.

Just need a little spit and polish, he thought with a wide smile. And he would show his future mate just how much she meant to him.

Yes, his Stallion whinnied, *mine*.

Chapter Eight

The sound of yelling and feet stomping through the halls brought Furio out of his work-induced daydreaming.

His mind often drifted while he cut wood, hammered nails, and put together the perfect second floor loft for his *piccolina*. Jessenia was a Witch, and he had his suspicions the title kitchen was going to be dropped after her powers had kicked his ass earlier that week.

It had been days since he'd seen her, but he knew she was still there. Could catch her fresh basil scent in the halls. And okay, so maybe he'd been spying on her from afar. He couldn't help it.

Now that he had publicly announced she belonged to him, his Stallion was more possessive than ever. The beast wanted her claimed, and he did not understand how building a loft was going to achieve that.

But Furio knew better. At least, he thought he did. Sure, he could seduce her. And that thought humbled him, but he did not want her to feel tricked in any way.

This was a labor of love, and he hoped to achieve one thing only with it. And that was her happiness. Provided she accepted him as mate, Furio would get the chance to make her happy for a very long time. Something he looked forward to with relish.

If not, well, he didn't want to think about it. In fact, he couldn't. His Stallion would not allow him to entertain thoughts of failure, though he supposed at the very least he could move out of the room. Give it to her since it only made sense if she was living there. But he was really fucking hoping he would not have to.

When he looked up, he wasn't at all surprised to see over a dozen hours had passed since he last checked. He was tired, but curious. No one ever ran around the hallways in the Keep. It was too dangerous. The corridors could and would continue forever if you didn't have a clear destination in mind.

Designed that way to keep intruders and

burglars busy for hours or sometimes longer, until one of the Guardians returned to free them or send them on their way to the local Enforcers. Spells and similar wards and enchantments were used to protect the ancient castle and all who lived there.

Kinda cool. Furio had been doing some reading about the place. It was slow-going because of his dyslexia, but he wanted to know more about it before he'd started his project. Understanding the fundamentals of the magic used to create the Keep was important. Good thing Holley was there. He'd sought her out in his efforts to win Jessenia and she'd recommended the book. Even helped make it more accessible by bespelling a pair of glasses to help correct his dyslexia.

"A dyslexic brain is not a broken brain," the sassy Witch had told him firmly, *"It should have been identified by your teachers when you were young. But no worries, I have just the thing."*

For the first time ever, Furio laughed about his hidden problem. He'd accepted the glasses and promised to seek her out should he have any more trouble.

All Shifters had inherent powers that allowed them to share their bodies and souls with an animal half, but most, like him, were wary of actual magic.

The kind of magic Jessenia had used to nearly suffocate him was scary as fuck. But at the time, he'd deserved an ass whopping.

More yelling sounded in the halls, and he knew he had to see what was up. He stood and wiped his hands on his jeans, grabbing a flannel along the way. Comfortable with his nudity didn't mean running around naked. His Stallion had been pretty fucking picky about that lately as well. He wanted one person's eyes on him, and until he had her, he'd prefer Furio to stay buttoned up.

Mincha. He rolled his eyes and shrugged the shirt on, snagging the vegan leather thong he used to keep his hair back from the dresser. He opened his door, and damn near bowled Storm over in the process.

"Shit," he grimaced, "You okay? What's goin' on?"

"It's Holley," he said, and for the first time in memory, the Wolf Shifter looked scared.

"Something is wrong with the young," he whispered, as if saying the thing aloud would make it true.

"Fuck," Furio cursed.

He felt as if someone punched him right in the gut. Shifter pregnancies were fragile and dangerous at best. Holley was a Witch, but her mate was Dragon. If any supernatural had a low birth rates, it was surely those rare, fantastical beasts.

"Come on," Storm slapped him on the arm, "Kingston wants us to meet him in his study."

A few seconds later, and they were inside the familiar room where Kingston conducted most of the business side to his Guardian duties. The man looked haggard and as scared as Furio had ever seen him.

"Where is she?" Byram whispered, moving next to their leader.

"In our bedroom," he grunted, "Jessenia, Fergie, and Elena are helping her into bed."

"What happened?" Furio whispered, but in a room of Shifters and other supes, that was kinda pointless.

"Shhh," Storm scolded, and the look he gave him would've turned a lesser man to stone.

As it was, Furio shook it off. It might not be his place to speak up, asking about their Alpha's mate, but fuck it. Even after the way he'd responded to Kingston's mating, he cared dammit.

"Why is he here?" Egros asked.

Maybe he didn't have a right. Maybe he didn't even deserve to be in that room with the rest of the

Guardians, but he would support his Alpha. Despite his past actions, he was still a Guardian. *Always.*

"Quiet," Byram hissed, "This is not about any of you," he said and watched his leader turn back around to face them.

Someday he would earn their trust back. He would prove his worth, and his loyalty to their group of Guardians. He'd thought he was forgiven, but Shifters were pretty dang serious when it came to mates. His trespasses were severe, and he might not ever gain back the same regard he'd had prior to his stupidity.

It's your own damn fault, he reminded himself, and kept his mouth shut for the duration.

No, they weren't all privy to his past. They did not all know about how he came to be there. The way Kingston had picked him up from the orphanage, and the way Neela had welcomed the teenaged Shifter with the chip on his shoulder the size of Morris County.

He'd seen the she-Dragon as a mother figure. And yeah, he'd felt betrayed when he'd learned the truth with the rest of them. But they wouldn't know about that either. He wasn't some pansy-ass motherfucker who needed to explain his feelings with them.

No fucking way. His Stallion snorted, taking

offense at the suggestion. He did his best to placate the beast. Yes, it pained him to think he'd lost his place with them, but he'd made his bed, now he'd lie in it.

What choice was there? Furio had no use for whining. He would face what he had coming to him like a man. But he still cared, dammit. Whether they believed him or not, he cared about Holley, Kingston, and their young.

"Holley woke up to some spotting and cramps," the Dragon explained between gritted teeth,

This was difficult for him to say. Fuck, it was difficult to hear. Holley was not only new to their circle, but she'd been in some kind of magical suspension for centuries. None of them knew what that meant or how it would affect her pregnancy. Still, Furio's heart wrenched at the words his Alpha spoke.

"She is worried, we both are. Egros called a healer, but he will not be here for at least a day," he ran a hand over his face.

The tension in the air was thick and heavy. No one moved, or even breathed. Suddenly, the sound of the bedroom door cracking open had everyone turning. Without seeing, he knew instinctively who was there.

Furio's heart began to thud inside his chest. It

was Jessenia. She looked worried. Her normally jovial expression was replaced by something else. Fear, empathy, and determination.

"She is resting now," Jessenia said to Kingston.

Her eyes swept the room and landed on him for a moment. She took a deep, calming breath as she approached the room full of powerful Guardians. And still her gaze came back to his, seeming to take strength in his presence.

Fuck. That felt good, he realized. He nodded slightly, hoping to reassure her. Her eyes widened, but she looked away far too soon. As if catching herself.

"Thank you," Kingston nodded, barely holding on to his control, "What else can we do for her? Do you know of anything?"

"Actually, that's why I left the bedroom just now. You see, Holley, and I were talking about some temporary remedies that might work. Things to help sustain a Shifter pregnancy. I know of at least one tea that could help. She agrees it might, but the ingredients can only be gathered at certain times," she hesitated, "and under certain conditions."

"I will do anything," Kingston said, "just tell me-"

"You can't, Kingston. You have to stay here, with

her. Only a woman can gather what I need to make this tea-"

"So, Elena then?" the Dragon asked.

"No," Jessenia licked her lips, and Furio watched the byplay with more than passing interest, "I have to be the one."

"I can't ask you to put yourself at risk," the Dragon shook his head, and Furio felt relief rush through him.

He was smart enough to keep his fucking mouth shut, but it was a near thing. The idea of her being in harm's way sent his Stallion into a rage. The Loyalists had been quiet lately, but that was nothing to go by. They could be plotting something. No, she was better off inside the Keep. But his relief was short-lived.

"Don't worry," she said, and nodded at his Alpha "I can and will do this."

Fucking hell. His Stallion whinnied, stomping his feet with his ears pressed back tight against his head. Agitated was not exactly the word to describe how his animal felt. Angry as fuck fit better. And yet, he knew if he said one word, he would damage whatever truce they'd had going over the last few days.

"Okay," Kingston said in the background, "But what are the special circumstances?"

Jessenia looked around the room. The tart scent of her embarrassment reached Furio. He frowned as others stared openly at the little kitchen Witch. Egros cleared his throat. Clearly, the guy had some idea, but he simply averted his gaze when Furio stared at him in question. What the hell was going on? He wondered, anxiety starting to rise.

"Well, the remedy requires ingredients gathered from the forest. Bark from a mature Black Cherry tree, to be exact. It can only be harvested under the light of the full moon by a female Witch. Preferable the one who plans to brew the healing tea," she hesitated again.

The scent of her embarrassment set his Stallion on edge. But his curiosity was also truly piqued. What was she hiding exactly?

"Tonight, is the full moon, and it's already eleven o'clock. I have to leave soon to find the right tree. I have to do it before midnight, so I can harvest at the exact time the clock strikes-"

"I know where a Black Cherry tree stands, I can fly you there," Kingston said, but before he could protest, Jessenia shook her head.

"No, I have to walk," she shook her head, "it's part of the sacrifice required to balance the spell.

And yes, Holley told me you'd both seen one a few months ago, I know where to go."

"It's too dangerous," Furio said aloud, and receive matching glares from everyone in the office.

He didn't give a fuck. Jessenia was precious to him. He had to say something.

"I will be fine," she hissed in his direction.

"She is right," Egros added.

Kingston's head swiveled to where the male Witch stood. And everyone else's did too. Only Furio remained unmoved. His eyes remained fixed on the pair of rich brown beauties that were currently attempting to drive daggers through him.

Shit.

"Of course, I'm right," she snapped, then took a deep breath before continuing, "I'm a kitchen Witch, but I know my stuff, okay? I have to do this alone."

"Alright," Kingston nodded sharply, "But Jessenia, she is my life. If anything were to happen to her, I don't know what-"

"It will be okay, Kingston," Byram nodded, "the little kitchen Witch knows her stuff."

The seemingly casual remark made Furio both growl and gnash his teeth. The Vampire seemed delighted at his response, which made his Stallion even more pissed. The beast snorted in warning.

Then Jessenia moved, and his attention was fully on her. She exhaled and straightened her shoulders. Giving him one scathing look before leaving the room.

Byram's smile grew wider, and he bowed at Jessenia as she passed him. Furio snorted again. Out loud. He didn't like the Vampire's overly familiar grin. He liked even less that it had been directed towards his mate.

Fuck. She wasn't his yet. He had to remember that. But he could not stop himself from caring about her. Something was definitely up, and he needed to find out what.

Following her path along the corridor, he kept his destination in mind. Trying to catch up with the surprisingly fleet of foot Witch was not all that difficult. He was a Stallion, after all. Keeping her in mind was not difficult either.

Jessenia. Yes, that part was easy enough, but once confronted with her closed bedroom door, Furio started to sweat. He didn't have time to think about what to do or say.

Mincha! Furio's Stallion butted against his skin. His animal wanted out, wanted her, but he reined him in tightly. Wiping his suddenly damp palms on his jeans, he stood up straight the second he heard the knob click. The door opened, and the scent of sweet, fresh-picked basil tickled his senses.

There she was. His gorgeous *piccolina*. Delightfully flushed and wearing a floor-length hooded cloak. Wait, what? Had he missed something? Was Halloween twice this year? Eyes roving over the thin black garment, his lips pursed tightly when they came to her bare feet.

"What are you doing here?" she asked, and he detected a familiar note of annoyance in her voice.

Shit. Choosing to ignore it, he decided to go with the obvious. He gestured to her clothes with his hands.

"What are you wearing?"

Cocking his head to the side, he realized that was the wrong question. The right one would have been, what wasn't she wearing?

"Nothing," she said, "and don't try to stop me."

Her face burned a brighter shade of red as she stepped forward, pushing past him in the process.

"Wait, Jess," he said.

He wanted to try to explain. To offer his help. But she was moving so dang quickly. Like she couldn't even stand to be in the same space as him.

Shit. That was his own damn fault. He should just let her go. Was resolved to do just that, but his hand shot out as if of its own accord, and he stopped her.

"Furio," she gasped.

That's when he noticed a flash of pale skin where the two sides of the long, black garment suddenly parted. The fuck?

"You're naked!" he shouted.

Cursing roundly, he moved fast. Had to block her from view since he heard footsteps sneaking up on them, and fast.

"Uh, what's going on here?" Fergie asked, her arm looped through Storm's.

The couple was probably headed towards the kitchen. Looking for snacks, he hazarded a guess. But Furio was beyond speech at the moment. He was growling loudly.

The angry sound reverberated through his chest as his Stallion stomped and snorted. The beast was tearing him up on the inside.

"Knock it off, Furio," she said, but he stepped closer.

Blocking her entirely with his tall, wide frame, he was about a second from freaking out. Well, what was he supposed to do? His mate was naked in the hallway, and there were others present.

Her small hands pressed against his chest, and

his animal whinnied. He wished like hell she was touching him for another reason, but he'd still take it. Dog that he was.

"Greetings everyone," Byram said.

Great, another fucking person joined them, and his Stallion was about to burst through his skin. The animal understood what was happening on a level best described as basic.

His mate was nude in the hallway where anyone could see her. And the suddenly murderous beast had one response.

Hell fucking no.

Chapter Nine

Jessenia closed her eyes as wave after wave of embarrassment, and humiliation threatened to drown her. She'd barely gotten out of Kingston's office with her secret, but here she was.

Butt ass naked in the hallway with the one freaking Guardian she'd been avoiding all week. Crap. She would so rather not have to explain this to him, of all people.

She'd been reading about Shifters and their mates. Understood a little better that like it or not, his animal was going to be like batshit crazy jealous over until they formally mated. And maybe even after.

Sigh. Some people got their kicks off of jealous

significant others, but Jessenia had almost little to no experience with it. She just didn't inspire jealousy.

Hell, she was a mousy little kitchen Witch with a big mouth, a fat ass, and a love of bookish things. What could she say? She was average at best.

"Fucking perfect," he growled, pressing his nose to the crux of her neck.

She yelped at the press of his hard, *and yes, she meant hard*, and hot, *oh boy, very, very hot, like smokin' hot* body against hers. The stone wall was cold, but she hardly felt it from the inferno coming off him.

"Um, guys? You need to keep walking or *Mr. Ed* here is gonna go ape-shit," Jessenia nodded at Storm and Fergie, who she knew was about to protest.

"But-"

Fergie yelped. *Sigh.* Luckily, Storm bent down and propped his mate over his shoulder, hustling her out of the hallway while she tried to get the situation under control.

"Mine," Furio growled again.

The word shouldn't have sent spikes of desire shooting straight to her core, but they did. *Oh yeah, they really did.* She could feel her needy sex throb and grow slick with want of him.

Great. Now she had to go traipsing through the forest with the female version of blue balls.

What the hell even was that? Blue ovaries? Blue nipples? Whatever. Fucking fabulous.

"No!" she scolded, "Bad horsey!"

"What?"

The slap to his ass seemed to prompt him to lift his head. He looked shocked, but also a tad bit interested. Dammit. That only turned her on even more.

"Listen, *Pony Boy*, I have to go," she pushed against his check.

"Pony boy?" he looked confused.

Oh well. She had to say something to shake him up. Poor guy was vibrating with emotion. He had the most big, hard, *oooh*, make that *very big and hard* body, pressed up against hers. His hands were on the wall behind her head and she was positive, he'd left a dent.

She shoved slightly and he moved back a step. Okay, so she immediately missed his incredible warmth and strength, but she wouldn't be admitting that aloud. Not anytime soon, anyway.

"I have to go," she said.

"You aren't wearing any clothes."

"That's right."

"Jessenia, why aren't you wearing clothes?"

He tried for calm. She could see it in the way he controlled his breathing, and she silently applauded the effort. Jessenia knew enough about Shifters now to understand this was tough on him.

Not that he deserved her consideration. After all, the man had lied to her. By omission, but still, it counted. The question in his dark green eyes was begging for a response, and she felt her resolve wavering.

Dang it. Jessenia always was a big softy at heart. She couldn't help herself. The way his jaw was clenched tight, and the furrows in his brow made her want to reach out and soothe his Stallion.

The nostrils at the end of his straight, Roman nose flared in his angst, and she clenched her fists lest she throw herself at him. Literally.

Fine. Maybe she should give him a break. Even if it was kinda nice seeing him all worked up over her. He was the one who'd been denying what they were to each other for freaking months now. Leaving her wondering why she wanted him so badly, and he hardly seemed interested.

"I am a Witch, Furio. You know that, right?"

"Yeah, but you usually wear clothes," he grunted.

"True," she said, and he did have a point, "Holley needs my help. Her baby is in distress, and only a special tea brewed from the bark of a Black Cherry tree can help her while we wait for the healer to come. In order to get the right magical benefits from the tree bark, I have to harvest it a certain way," she felt her face heat.

"You also have no shoes on," he frowned.

"Yep," she nodded, "No clothes, and no shoes. I can't wear them. At all. The cloak's just until I get outside."

"No," he growled.

"Yes."

"I don't like it," he tried again.

"Well, too bad for you," she scoffed.

"You'll freeze," Furio shook his head, causing his hair to ripple on either side of his face as it came loose from its tie, "and it's not safe."

"I'll be okay," she argued, somewhat fascinated by his glossy locks.

Honestly, Jessenia was frightened. Holley had been attacked just outside the Keep. Offner was gone now, that was true, but his followers were still at large.

The Loyalists had tried separating themselves from their former leader's radical fanaticism, but they were not exactly known for their fine judgement. Wanting to control magic was as unnatural as wanting to control the tides. It was just not the order of things. Magic was wild and wonderful. It could be used for bad, but in its most basic form it was a thing of beauty. But only if free.

The Guardians' creed came to mind, and she smiled, reciting the words in her brain. From chaos comes creation. Yes, indeed.

But she was not a Guardian. Nor was she a *conpar*. Not yet, maybe not ever. What if the Loyalists were watching them now? Shivers of fear raced down her spine, but she shook them off.

A naked kitchen Witch would be a sitting duck. But she was still going. Jessenia couldn't fail in her mission. Holley needed her, and besides, she was made of stronger stuff than anyone knew. Even her.

"I am going with you," he said, and for a moment gratitude flowed through her.

Jessenia wasn't a warrior, but she believed in the Guardians of Chaos. She supported their cause as her own. Deep inside her Witch's heart she knew without a doubt that fighting for the freedom of all magic was what she was supposed to do.

Even a kitchen Witch could turn the tide. She had more than enough self-respect to know that. It was like her grandmother always said, everyone had a role to play in this world.

Furio's expression booked no argument, so she nodded. Thankful he was going with her if for no other reason than to ensure the job got done without incident.

"Okay."

"You're saying yes?" he looked shocked.

She ignored him, putting one foot in front of the other. Jessenia managed to not fall on her face as she reached the back door. Before she could touch the handle, he was there.

Opening the door for her, one hand outstretched as if he wanted to place it on the small of her back but didn't dare touch. Regret welled up, but she pushed it away. Their story was not over yet.

The future could still be theirs, maybe if they were both willing to exchange in a little give and take. She stood still for a moment and tried to gain her courage. Her feet were frozen on the cold stone patio. It stretched only a dozen or so feet beyond the Keep, and after that, a thick blanket of white snow covered the ground.

"Are you sure about this?"

His question was quiet, low, like a whispering wind fleeting through her mind. Jessenia sucked in a deep breath and nodded. She cared very much about

Holley and Kingston, about all of them. She would help. If she could, she would. Period.

"I am sure," she said, "They're my friends. I would do anything to help a friend."

With nothing to prove to anyone but herself, Jessenia inhaled one more cold fortifying breath. She knew her limitations as a Witch, but this was medicine she'd studied with her grandmother. This was a magic old as time itself.

Treatments normals now ignored in favor of big pharma. No one appreciated the sacrifice and creative forces that went into healing anymore. The first Witches were healers, midwives, that kind of thing.

But they were few and far between these days. Witches were the only species of supernatural that were ever well and truly outed throughout all of time. And no one was despised more, except maybe the Devil himself.

"You will let me walk with you the whole way? I'll keep you safe," the latter was more statement than question, but she found herself nodding at him.

He might have denied her in the beginning, but he was here now. His animal was pushing him hard, somehow, she could tell, but for whatever reason,

Jessenia was willing to take it. She did not want to do this alone.

"Okay," she said, "but you can't interfere. Promise?"

Her eyes bore into his, she saw the hesitation, the questions in the glittery green pools, but she wasn't about to address them. Their relationship was on rocky grounds as it was.

Maybe they could have a future. Somehow, someway, but she couldn't rightly tell. Precognition wasn't one of her kitchen Witch's powers. Furio seemed to study her passively, and she let him. Pretty soon there would be nothing between them. Literally.

Jessenia had to fight her nerves to control the shaking of her limbs as she turned to face the path that led straight to the heart of the barrens. Her hands trembled as she undid the ties that held the cloak together.

Getting naked in front of a man, any man, was never easy for a woman like Jessenia. She knew she was cute, but that didn't mean self-consciousness abandoned her at any given time during her life.

A realist, she knew all too well that being vertically challenged with average-sized breasts, a bigger than she'd have liked butt, and a soft belly put her squarely in the *okay* range on the hotness meter. And she didn't even want to think about her thick thighs and other jiggly bits.

Sigh. The fact she'd been lusting after the man she was about to strip in front of, and not for any fun-time reason, only made her more nervous. But it was too late to back out now.

Besides, Holley needed her, and she would not let her friend down. Jessenia sucked in some cold air and grabbed her metaphorical balls, then dropped the cloak. Ignoring his sharp intake of breath, she took the first step forward into the cold night.

"I'd say it's colder than a witch's titty, but that would be too self-deprecating even for me," she tried to make light of the situation, but was met with only silence.

A moment later she knew why. Jessenia turned her head to glance at her escort, only to be greeted by the sounds of cloth being ripped and torn. Next came the telltale cracking and stretching sounds of bones and muscles breaking and re-knitting.

Gasping at what she'd never realized was obviously a painful process, Jessenia stopped and stared in wonder. The air shimmered with green ethereal lights surrounding his body and whirling in a fury of activity. It was incredible, beautiful, and something

Shifters rarely shared with anyone else except maybe in the heat of battle.

The lights dimmed, and he was there. Smelling like sunshine and spring breezes, even though it was near midnight and no more than twenty-degrees outside. Then Furio was standing beside her. Only, it wasn't him exactly.

It was his Stallion. The magnificent beast whinnied and shook his head, sending his glossy mane shimmering in the moonlight. She'd never seen his imposing steed before.

The Italian Draft Horse was an incredible animal. He was enormous, with a shiny white coat that looked like a bolt of glittery satin in the darkness. His mane and tail were both long and dark, like his own ebony locks.

Breathtaking and powerful, but not at all like the racehorses she'd seen on TV. She knew instinctively he was built for more than speed or entertainment. No, nothing so frivolous as that.

His beast was designed to conquer. A true warhorse. Nineteen hands high, and over eighteen-hundred pounds of pure muscle and strength. His enormous head nudged her, as if to say go, and she did. Shivering once she realized where she was and what she was doing.

"We better hustle," she said aloud, knowing he understood her even in this shape.

Furio kept pace beside her, blocking the wind from chilling her further with his enormous body. Who was she kidding? Temperatures were already dropping, but he gave off heat like a furnace and she was grateful though her toes were numb as she stepped carefully on the ice and snow.

A noise like an animal scurrying sounded to the left, and she turned her head. It was nothing, but it sent her heart racing, and she stood still for a moment too long. Furio whinnied.

"I guess it was nothing," she whispered and placed a hand on his back for her comfort more than his.

With only a thin, steel blade in one hand, and her other secure on his tall back, she ambled forward. The pine forest was dark and imposing. The moonlight glinted off the snow, creating shadows and an atmosphere more suited to a horror film than reality.

Her breath made cloudy white puffs in the air, and she tried not to tremble, but it was part of her sacrifice she knew. Magic demanded that from her, and she gave it freely. The least she could do to help her friends was take a walk through the snow.

Still, she was scared. Jessenia was so much more

at home in the kitchen. Her magic practiced through cooking and baking with healing prayers, healthy wishes, love and positivity as her only intentions.

She wasn't going to deny her fear. That would negate her sacrifice all together and it might sully the magic. No, she acknowledged it, and that alone gave her strength and power.

It was a twenty-minute walk from there to where the stand of Black Cherry trees stood, and she was more grateful by the second for his company. The woods at night were beautiful on one hand. Stark and silent, the trees towered above them, over-whelming in their magnitude.

Holley had described the path in detail, but it was so very different up close. With the heavy snow-falls just lately, Jessenia found herself up to her ankles in some places. The pain of the freezing ground shot through to her bones, but she knew it was all part of it. It was the price required by the universe for the ritual to work.

Biting back her discomfort, Jessenia gritted her teeth, refusing to give in to the cold. She kept on going, the gently snorts and chuffs from Furio's Stallion kept her mind from wandering too far.

Everything took on a sort of silvery luster beneath the enormous moon and its bright, glowing light. She was taken back by the pure beauty of her home state. She loved it there, never wanted to leave it.

New Jersey wasn't all concrete cities. It was mountains, forests, beaches, and trails. It was magic and moonlight. A hub of supernatural activity. And she was part of that world.

Even if she was just a kitchen Witch.

Chapter Ten

"There," Jessenia's whisper cut through the silence like the steel blade she carried in her grip.

In her excitement, she was not paying attention. Suddenly, she stumbled over some tangled tree roots the snow had hidden from her sight. The air hummed and shimmered with magic as Furio returned to his human form. His arms reached out to snag her before she could hit the cold ground, but she shook her head.

"No," she shouted, and braced herself for the fall.

"Fuck! Are you okay?" he reached for her again, but she shied away, and lifted herself off the cold snowy ground.

"Jessenia?"

"I'm fine," she breathed, and shook the snow off her skin.

She only thanked the gods she'd dropped the blade first. Otherwise, it might be embedded somewhere entirely uncomfortable. Like her very cold, very pink skin.

"You're freezing, *piccolina*," he growled, and something about the pet name he called her made her warm inside.

"It's okay," she got the words out between her chattering teeth, as she looked through the snow to find the blade.

Once in hand, she approached the tall Black Cherry. Well, shit. Of course, it was gigantic. And she, being herself, could barely reach a branch.

"Fucking hell," he grunted, but she ignored him, "it's not even midnight yet. You'll never make it if I don't get you warm."

"Can't," she shivered, "Have to sacrifice for the magic to work-"

"You sacrifice too much, *piccolina*," he reached for her again, and this time, there was no stopping him.

With one hand on her waist and the other on her

neck, he pulled her forward into the circle of his arms.

Oh my. He was like a furnace. Her body shivered in delight at the warmth of his touch. Smooth skin, rippling muscles, and that springtime scent were driving her mad. Anticipation flowed through her, making her weak with need to the point where she lifted her face, sighing in relief when he bent his head.

Furio whispered her name reverently, almost hopefully, then their lips met, and she could hardly think. Walls closed in on them until they were the only two beings in the universe. Jessenia gave in to the moment. That kiss was a promise. She felt it as real as the soft stubble that graced his cheeks and chin. The steady pressure of his lips on hers was intoxicating.

She relaxed against him, opening her mouth just wide enough for his tongue to invade. Thrilling wasn't a word she'd ever used to describe a man, but it was how she felt in his arms.

He was that and more. He was adventure. He was comedy, safety, and desire. Tantalizing and captivating. Strong, willful, proud, and yet tender, giving, and so damn sweet.

She wanted more. She wanted it all. But did he

truly want her? That was the real question. The evidence of his carnal interest was currently pressed against her belly, and she had no doubt the two of them would set the bed on fire.

At the moment, she knew it more a question of when rather than if. Jessenia moaned softly, but no other sounds except the beating of their hearts, and their racing pulses made it to her ears.

Everything seemed to fall away as she kissed him back. Her arms were pinned inside his embrace making her his prisoner in effect. But she was not afraid of him. She had never felt safer or more protected than with him.

Before she was ready, Furio ended the kiss. Pressing his forehead to hers, he breathed like it was something difficult. And she somehow realized, it was. He didn't want to let her go, and the knowledge of that warmed her like nothing else could.

"Feeling warmer?" he cut through her reverie, and she closed her eyes as the timber of his voice rolled through her like hands stroking her skin.

"Yeah," she nodded, and pressed her lips to his chastely once more.

"It's midnight, *piccolina*," he whispered.

Jessenia wanted to curse. Hell, she really wanted to stay right where she was, but she had a job to do.

Turning around to face the old cherry tree, Jessenia raised her arms high. Chanting the words Holley taught her, she began to slice pieces of near-frozen bark from the trunk.

The wood was hard to cut through, but her knife was sharp and her aim accurate. Sometimes it paid to be a good cook. She hacked at the wood, collecting the bits in her palm.

Next, she moved to the branches nearest her, cursing herself for her own lack of height. Bark from the trunk and branches both were necessary.

"Climb on my back," Furio said from so close behind her, his breath tickled her neck.

"I d-don't know," her teeth chattered.

"I'll shift and kneel down. Climb on my back, *piccolina*, and you can reach the branch. Let me help you, let me help Holley. I think you've suffered enough for balance. Besides, I'm the one sacrificing my back to your ice cube feet," he joked.

His voice was so deep, and his words attractive. She knew they were meant to help, but Jessenia wasn't going to risk it. She was going to do this old school. And little did he know, but having him there was giving her the strength to do all this when all she wanted was to curl into a ball and let the cold overcome her.

"Just stay with me," she whispered back, "I can do this, I know I can."

"Of course, you can," he said, as if that was obvious.

Jessenia smiled then, and it hurt her poor, frozen face, but she couldn't help it. That was the Furio she'd grown so fond of. The one who stated the most outrageous things as if they were evident to all.

Jessenia jumped up and grabbed the end of the branch. Pulling it down with all her might, she ignored the sting of the frozen snow that fell and hit her naked skin. Struggling with the knife to whittle off more bits of bark and some twigs as well, she concentrated on the task at hand.

All the while, she was keenly aware of his eyes on her. Even as she'd chanted the spell Holley taught her, Jessenia knew her Stallion kept watch. Protecting her.

Once she'd collected enough, she turned to see Furio still standing on two feet. Uncaring of his own nudity, he simply waited. An imposing, yet steady presence that bulked her spirit.

His hair hung in a dark tangle down his back, and she wondered if he had any idea how good-looking he was. Of course, he probably did. But really, she found herself tongue tied.

He looked like he belonged to another time. With his chiseled features, cords of rippling muscles, tall frame, and naturally bronzed skin, he could have been a Spartan soldier, or a Roman legionnaire. Maybe a gladiator fighting lions with his bare hands.

"Are you finished?" he asked, looking at her curiously while she stared like some lovesick teen.

"You didn't shift?" she asked, shaking herself out of her own stupor.

"Nah, if you walk, I walk."

"But before you-" she started.

"Before my Stallion took over before I could control myself. It seemed better to allow him to have his way."

"I don't understand. Why couldn't he control himself?"

"Jessenia," he snorted, "You're naked."

He said it as if it explained everything. She looked down at her puckered nipples that tipped medium-sized breasts, the soft belly beneath them, wide hips, and the dark curls that covered her sex. Short legs and red, cold feet followed. Hardly beautiful, but he was staring like he couldn't get enough.

"So?"

"Do you even know how gorgeous you are? How

much work I find myself having to do not to reach out and grab you right this fucking second?"

"Oh, come on. You're not a teenager, Furio, and I know my physical limitations."

"You really have no idea how drop-dead gorgeous you are right now?"

"I am not the first woman you've seen naked," she scoffed.

"Jessenia, you are the only woman that matters to me," he said as the Keep came into view, "When are you going to believe me when I tell you that I want you? I always want you. You're my fated mate, and even if you weren't, *piccolina*, I would still want you."

Her heart was pounding in her chest as his emerald green eyes bore down into hers. Before she could utter a single reply, two things happened.

First, a group of men dressed in black leapt out at them from the shadows, and second, Furio kissed her hard and fast, before pushing her towards the Keep.

"Jessenia! Run!"

Chapter Eleven

Bespelled iron shackles bit into his wrists, but Furio refused to utter a sound as the group of Loyalists shoved him into his cell.

"Fucking Guardian filth!"

"Look at this bastard! Thinks he can tell us what to do!"

"Traitor to your kind!"

"Get in there before we turn you into glue!"

He'd heard shit like that all his life, and it was easy enough to shake off. The back of his head still throbbed from the blitz attack, but he did what he had to do to keep their focus on him. He'd almost gone fucking nuts thinking about what they would do to Jessenia if they caught her.

His Stallion raged at him, battling against the

group of Shifters until he saw his mate haul her sweet little ass out of there. Thank fuck. The group of armed-to-the-teeth Loyalist fuckers had been so focused on getting him secured, she'd flitted right through their trap.

He should have known better. Should've been paying attention, but that was pretty difficult when his mate was parading around in the freezing cold in her birthday suit. And what a suit it was.

Mincha! He could die a happy man right then, having seen the heaven he would surely find one day in her sweet embrace.

No fucking way. His Stallion snorted and stomped. The animal within him was in no way, shape or form going to allow him to even entertain thoughts of death. Not when his *piccolina* was out there needing him.

She might be pissed off at him for being a jerk, but she was his. And now they both knew it. Furio couldn't exactly blame her for being pissed at him, and he would readily accept it and apologize every day of his life forever now that he knew she wanted him too.

Fucking a. The sassy little kitchen Witch had shown him how much with the sweet, desperate way she'd returned his kiss. Both kisses.

Rrrr. His Stallion growled and snorted. The beats wanted out. He wanted to find her. Now. Was pissed as hell Furio hadn't claimed her when in all the months he'd known her.

Restraint was hard for a guy like him, but for her, he would wait forever. And he'd prove it too as soon as he got the fuck out of this mess. She was worth it. Hell, she was worth everything. Furio closed his eyes, mumbling a quick prayer for her safety. There were some things that were simply ingrained in a man.

Growing up in a Catholic orphanage meant praying came naturally to him despite everything he disagreed with about organized religion. He always felt a certain peace come over him whenever he spoke to God, or the gods, and yes, he prayed to both.

It was all the same to him. And he would continue to pray to any and all if they would just make sure *she* was safe. It was incredible, and a little crazy, to think how fucking stupid he'd been to deny his feelings.

But he understood now that he loved her. Had since the day they met. He should kick himself in the head for delaying claiming the beautiful female. Stupid self-pity. It didn't matter if he thought he was worth it, she did and that was all that mattered.

Besides, Furio was a good man. He would work his ass off to deserve her. Now that he'd had a small taste, he wanted more. Hell, he wanted it all. His Jessenia was sassy as fuck.

Bellissima, molto bellissima. So fucking beautiful. Rrrr.

Watching her cut a path through the snow, her gorgeous womanly shape had him so hard he could barely stand up straight. But it was more than her body that enticed the beast. Hell, he loved every inch of her inside and out. Especially the way her big brown eyes lightened to amber when he kissed her.

She had such a big, beautiful heart. Pure gold was how he'd describe her to anyone who asked. Even the damp, dark cell he was currently chained to couldn't dim his feelings for the woman.

The reality of his situation sucked, but it was temporary. Hell fucking yeah, it was. Unlike his feelings for his *piccolina*. He would get out, and he would go to her. Claim her as his own.

Yes, his Stallion stomped in approval. The beast was desperate to give his mark to the woman. She his true and fated mate. Her and no other.

Shit. He had it bad, but that fact only made him grin wider. He loved everything about her. He could admit it now. Well, to himself anyway. This crazy thing he felt was more than just fate, it was love. And she thought he was upset about it, that he wouldn't choose her freely.

His fault, he knew. But he would make it up to her. If it took the rest of his life. For months he'd watched her. Learned everything he could about the little kitchen Witch.

She was honest and bright, practical, and silly too. Her laughter was the best damn sound he'd ever heard. Rich and earthy, like the wonderful concoctions she crafted in the kitchen.

She was one hell of a cook, and yeah, he'd noticed her dishes taking on a much more vegetarian aspect since she'd moved in. Hope blossomed at the realization she'd been doing that for him. Just another reason to survive whatever these fuckers had in store for him.

In all her interactions with the Guardians, Fergie, and Holley too, Jessenia proved to be kind and loving. She gave everything one hundred and ten percent. Look how she'd volunteered to walk naked through the forest in the middle of the night in February to gather the ingredients needed for a magical tea to help protect Holley and Kingston's pregnancy.

In-fucking-credible. Pride flowed through him at

her selfless act. But fuck, he shouldn't have let his guard down. Furio should have shifted to his Stallion and ran her sweet ass home.

He couldn't help the thrill that raced through him at the thought of her mounted on his Stallion's broad back. She'd hug his sides with her thighs and tug on his mane while he whisked her through the pines and snow-covered forest.

Even better, he thought of his sexy little *piccolina* astride his naked body, taking him deep inside her sweet body, while he took every care to ensure her pleasure and satisfaction.

Only yesterday, he would've doubted her desire for him, but today he knew better. He was ready to admit it and accept it. Hell, there was no denying it now. Need had sweetened her scent when he'd had the feisty little kitchen Witch wrapped up in his arms.

Just thinking about it made his cock hard and thick. He reached down and pinched himself, not wanting to be vulnerable considering where he was. A hard-on was damn inconvenient in these surroundings.

Mincha! He needed to find a way out. Needed to get back to her. To make sure she was safe.

Jessenia, his Stallion whispered inside his mind's

eye. He wished like hell for fiftieth time that hour, that he'd claimed her already. Maybe then he would know for sure if she was alright.

No, that was no way to think. She was safe.

She had to be.

Chapter Twelve

"Help!" Jessenia's voice rang through the kitchen as she used the back entrance to enter the Keep.

"What is it?" Byram came hurling into the room.

Thank goodness for his super-speed, she thought inanely. The movie star good looks of the Vampire would have caught her off guard once upon a time, but she knew him well enough by now. He was not for her. He was a friend. That was all.

Unmoved by his chiseled features and handsome face, she reached out as her frozen, stiff limbs met with the tiled floor. Byram stalled a moment, probably shocked at her nudity, and she fell to her knees.

"Jessenia!" he shouted.

Jessenia did not have time to worry about the Vampire, not when Furio was in danger. Stupid, stubborn Stallion. She closed her eyes as panic threatened to overwhelm her.

No, that was so not happening. She had to save him! Shaking from head to toe, she was grateful when Byram grabbed the tablecloth, wrapping it around her shoulders. He placed his hands on her arms, and she shied away from his touch, but recognized it as perfunctory.

Byram was only trying to help, she told her magic repeatedly. But it was as if the powers inside her refused the logic. That had never happened before, and she forced them to heed her will. She didn't want to hurt him.

"Ouch," he gritted his teeth when her powers shocked him.

"S-sorry," she mumbled between her chattering teeth.

He could help Furio, she told herself. That fact alone seemed to reassure her powers. Byram used his grip to help her stand, adjusting the cloth to preserve her modesty while he guided her to a chair.

"What happened? Jessenia?" he shook her shoulder gently.

Fuck, didn't he know she was trying hard not to

zap his ass? Her powers started to swirl and pulse, angry at his touch. She did not want his hands on her. They were wrong. *He* was wrong.

"Apologies," he bowed his head, and the Vampire smartly stepped away from her.

She dropped the Black Cherry tree bark she still had clutched in her palm on the table. Egros and Kingston had come running into the kitchen by then, followed by Storm and Fergie.

"Oh my God!" Fergie dropped to her knees by Jessenia's side, "Honey, are you alright?"

"W-we were amb-b-bushed. Please, we h-have to h-help F-Furio," she was shaking too hard to speak clearly, but they got the gist.

The moment they understood what she'd been trying desperately to convey, they started to make plans.

"I can't stay here," Kingston rubbed his face, "I have to help. Egros, can you and Jessenia make the tea for Holley?"

She knew it was difficult for the Dragon to leave his mate. But he assured her she was resting well and easy.

"Yes," Egros nodded, "Holley explained it all to me before she fell asleep," the male Witch began to gather other ingredients, and set them in a pot of boiling water to steep.

"Okay," Kingston was pointing to the place where Jessenia said they'd met with the enemy on an old map, "They must have taken him to the old hunter's cabin. Place is in ruins," he growled.

"G-get me clothes," she turned to Fergie, who nodded and ran down the hall to her room.

"No, you can't come with us. You aren't a Guardian, and besides, he'd want you here-" Storm said, but the look she flashed him as Fergie came back and held up a blanket so she could pull on a pair of leggings and top must've been more powerful than she'd thought.

The Wolf raised his hands in surrender and averted his gaze. Good. Last thing she wanted to do was freak out on her bestie's man, but she'd had enough of people telling her what she could and could not do.

First, Furio had made the decision to delay telling her she was his fated mate without any input at all. And now these fuckers thought they were leaving without her to save her man.

Hell no.

He'd sacrificed his own escape for her sake. She knew that, even though he would never admit to committing such a selfless act. But that was Furio. He never wanted praise. Despite his seemingly cocky attitude, he was shy about being in the limelight.

Something she understood all too well. Her vlog allowed her to connect with people, but it also held them at bay. She had all the power in that scenario. One click, and the connection could be severed.

But that wasn't the case with a mate, was it? No. It couldn't be that way. She would have to give up some of her power, her control. But the rewards, oh the rewards, would be worth it.

She only had to look at Fergie to understand that mating Storm was the most important decision her best friend had ever made. Truthfully, this was the happiest she had ever seen her. Even happier than during Nordstrom Rack's last shoe sale. And yes, Jessenia was thrilled for her, but she wanted some of that for herself.

With Furio. Images of her Stallion flitted through her mind. The thousand different ways he tried to tell her how he felt over the past few months, but she was too stubborn to see. He always held doors for her. Stole too many little glances to count. Whenever they went into town, he made sure she walked on the inside of the street.

He always took out the trash when she was finished cooking, and she'd caught him loading the dishwasher once or twice. He cared. And not just for her. But for every single one of them.

"Okay, you aren't getting rid of me. That Stallion is *my mate*. He put himself in danger to save *my butt*, so first," she grumbled, "we are rescuing his stubborn ass. Then, I'm going to kick it. And afterwards, I am going to claim him. Anyone have any objections?"

By the time she was finished, she was breathless. Green sparks seemed to shoot from her hands, and she was trembling, but not with cold. It was more like her powers were energized because they had a new purpose.

Find her mate and save his ass so she could kick it for putting her through this. Then maybe she could kiss it all better.

Yup. Solid plan.

"No problem here," Fergie grinned, elbowing Storm, who simply nodded his agreement.

Though Jessenia noticed, his eyebrows had somehow disappeared into his hairline.

"Sounds fair enough," Byram grinned.

"About time, little Witch," Elena smirked, "But how about I stay behind with Holley and Egros? That all right, Alpha?"

Kingston nodded at the Panther Shifter and closed his eyes. Probably communicating with his mate, Jessenia thought as she pulled on the heavy fleece Fergie had grabbed for her.

Next, she donned thick socks and waterproof boots. Finally, clothed and warm, she was ready. Kingston finished up discussing their plan of attack, and she listened intently. Her magic sparked at the opportunity to rescue her mate. Furio had been gone too long.

"Jessenia, can Egros do this?" Kingston turned and asked.

She saw the plea in his eyes but knew only the truth would do. The male Witch was not her biggest fan, and yet, he was honest and true to them all. He took his role as Guardian very seriously, and she admired the trait even if she didn't exactly like the man.

"Yes," she answered, after swallowing her surprise.

Egros was powerful, and he'd been a Guardian for decades. Surely, the Diamond Dragon trusted him. But that he should ask her, a mere kitchen Witch, meant a lot to Jessenia.

"Of course, he can do this. Egros, you good?" she asked, turning to watch as he measured out ingredients.

"I have everything I need," he stated in his usual quiet voice.

"Good. Let it steep for no more than ninety minutes. Then have her drink one full cup. You can save the rest for later. It will ease her discomfort and fortify her."

"Yes, I have been researching supernatural pregnancies," he told the room at large, "Seemed prudent in light of all the mates we seem to be acquiring just lately," he grinned, "Anyway, Dragonlings require triple the amount of nutrients, magical and natural, as other pregnancies. She simply needs more nourishment if you ask me, but I will check with the healer. He will be here on the hour."

"Makes sense," she smiled, surprised that the usually standoffish Witch had done so much work without telling anyone.

But that was Egros. Quiet and reliable. She looked forward to discussing more about his portals, after they used one to get them closer to the spot where Furio was more than likely being held.

He spoke with Kingston another minute, probably reassuring the Alpha of the Guardians that his mate would be okay.

"Are we ready?" Kingston asked.

Jessenia's heart thudded inside her chest. Now that she knew without a doubt that Furio was her mate, she wanted him more with every minute. Their relationship had developed slower than was usual for Shifter mates over the past few months, but it did not stop the rush of feelings that flooded her the moment the proverbial cat was out of the bag.

Her powers pulsed and hummed, as if seeking him out among those nearest. It missed him. Wanted him. Needed him. Now. But even then, she understood what it meant for Kingston to leave his own mate behind.

"Are you sure you want to go? He will understand if you stay with Holley," Jessenia began, but Kingston was already shaking his head.

"Furio is one of our own," he said in a gruff voice, "Holley has taken each of my Guardians, and their mates, under her wing. She will never forgive me if I let anything happen to him," he grinned, "Besides, Holley has everything she needs now, starting with that tea. Thank you for risking your life to get it," he said, eyes flashing with his Diamond Dragon.

"Okay," she swallowed hard, "Let's go get him."

Chapter Thirteen

Dammit. Running into these fuckers was just about the worst luck he'd ever had. And that was saying something.

Furio had had no choice. He growled as he strained against the cuffs. He'd needed to protect her. So, he practically offered himself up on a silver platter. Their group was made up of three Gila Shifters and two Rhinos. It was those big ass bastards that had finally taken him down.

Sure, he could've outrun them, but he wasn't willing to risk them getting to her. The precious moments it would have taken him to shift might have been too long to get her out safely.

So instead of trying, he'd slammed his lips to hers then shoved her in direction of the Keep with instructions to run. They'd been close enough for her to make it. And he'd made sure those fuckers' eyes were trained on him.

Five to one were just the kind of odds he liked, but he'd been distracted with thoughts of his mate. And they'd gotten him, eventually. Of course, he got his licks in too. Even now one big Rhino fuck was glaring at him through one almost closed eye, and a series of bruises and broken facial bones.

Furio grinned at the asshole. And the resounding growl only made him laugh. Fuck them and their efforts, he'd delivered one hell of a kick to that fucker's face if he did say so himself.

But now, they were not interested in fighting fairly. The sons of bitches were using magic. That sucked ass as far as he was concerned. Furio was more a fisticuffs kinda guy.

Judging from the glyphs and inky dark tendrils coming out of the thing, he figured it was dark magic. The bastards were up to no good, and the stink of lizard told him those freaks were remnants of the Gila Shifters who'd been in Offner's thrall.

"Is that the right spell?" one hissed.

Furio's Stallion whinnied in response. Horses were not predatory animals. Squashing his fight or flight instinct was difficult, but over the years he'd honed the fight part of his natural abilities.

Used in battle for thousands of years, his Stallion was genetically prone to stand his ground and stare the enemy in the eye. He never ran from a fight anymore. His beast more than able to engage with these assholes. Hell, he was ready for a rematch now.

Rrrr. The Stallion agreed.

"Shut up!"

The bastard threw something at the bars of the cell and the resounding ringing had him covering his ears.

Fucking dickhead.

He was too stupid to know it would hurt his brethren as well. The sound of someone punching the idiot's lights out was satisfying. He only wished it was him doing the honors.

"What is it you idiots think you're doing, anyway? You know I'm a Guardian, right? My team will come for me," he interrupted their little meeting, with his gravelly voice echoing in the small brick space.

Furio needed to identify where he was, to devise a plan, and that meant getting the morons to talk. He'd been knocked out with that blow to the head, but he knew he hadn't traveled very far. The scent told him he was still there, in the pine barrens.

For some reason, it was his experience that bad guys loved bullshitting about themselves. It was like they couldn't help it. Braggards and fools, the lot of them.

Standing up in his cell, he found he had to crouch because of the chains binding him. But as long as they were distracted, he could check for weakness in the links.

"I don't think so, *horse-breath*," a Shifter wearing black jeans and a gray thermal shirt laughed as he spat the words in Furio's direction, "You're on every-one's shit list, aren't you? They don't give a fuck about you."

"The fuck you say, dick lips?" he growled, but the words hurt.

"We've been watching you all for weeks. They avoid you like the fucking plague. You've pissed off your Alpha. Tried to come between him and his mate. They all hate you now," he sneered.

"You know nothing about us," Furio returned.

"I know enough," the one holding the grimoire turned to him, "Offner was single-minded, but he was right about the ley lines beneath that old castle. Once we get our hands on that plump Witch you were with, we can use her to gain control of it. You see, we have a plan," he remarked with the familiar fatal hubris of bad guys everywhere.

Dickheads, all of them, his Stallion thought with a whinny.

Still, there was that little seed of doubt threatening to plant itself inside of him. Were his Guardian brethren still mad at him for what he'd done? How he'd acted?

"No," he said aloud.

"No? Ha! As if you have a choice," the *soon-to-have- a horseshoe-shaped-dent-in-the-side-of-his-head-motherfucker* licked his lips.

He approached Furio's cell with all the cocksure mannerisms of a man who did not know he had moments to live. All this talk of Jessenia was making his animal eager for battle.

Horses might be vegetarians, but they were murderous sons of bitches when pushed. And this bastard had pushed him far enough.

"I saw your little whore Witch running on her chubby legs. Her bare-ass and tits jiggled with every step she took through those woods. Makes my dick hard just thinking about it. Don't worry, I'll have my cock buried in her cunt soon enough. You can bet on that, and with this grimoire, I will control her, and all magic. That's right, *me!*"

"Yeah? And just who the fuck are you?"

"What? You don't know me? I was Offner's right hand," he spat as he talked, but Furio managed not to blink.

"Sorry, you Lizard fuckers all smell the same to me."

"Well, when your friends come and find you dying, tell them it was me! Tell them that I, *Brian Thomas*, killed you!"

Furio grinned and reached through the bars of his cell, gripping Brian Thomas' neck in his hands while his buddies hollered and jumped out of the way as a ferociously loud roar sounded outside.

But they were not quick enough. Furio held onto the sonofabitch who'd threatened his mate, squeezing his neck until the man's eyes bugged out of his head.

He let go, Tossing the man's lifeless body to the ground, just in time to see *Brian* disappear under the crumbling brick and wood that gave way under a certain Diamond Dragon's massive stream of flame.

"What the?!" the Rhino Furio had kicked in the face yelped as more flames hit him right on the ass.

"Yes!" Furio laughed and rattled the cage he was in.

"Hey, Fur, you good?" yelled Storm.

The Stallion nodded, he'd never been so happy to see his friends in his life. But his joy was short-lived as the sounds of a certain kitchen Witch's bellow of rage met his ears.

"Jessenia!" he growled.

She was there? What the fuck!

His Stallion reared up inside of him. The idea that she might be injured or hurt in any way freaked him out completely. Beast and man both agreed, her safety was tantamount. His eyes glowed green, tinting everything in the same ethereal light. Or was that just his hands?

He whinnied aloud, pulling on the magicked cuffs they'd used to imprison him. Furio heard the Loyalists' crying out in pain, but it was not enough. He wanted them all to die just for thinking of hurting her.

Those fuckers deserved everything they got. Plotting against the supernatural world earned them a motherfucking beatdown. Plotting to hurt his mate? That earned them a death sentence.

Right then, he needed one thing and one thing only. To get to his mate. Snapping the chains with one last tug, he turned around and threw a mean back-kick towards the iron bars.

Shifting only his leg to his Stallion's powerful one, he barely grunted as the clang of his hoof breaking through the magicked metal echoed. It was music to his ears.

Once out of the cell, he saw his mate being manhandled by two Gila Shifters, and his vison went from green to red. Without even thinking about it, Furio shifted from his human shape to his enormous Stallion faster than he'd ever managed before. Only something was different.

"Holy shit, Furio," Storm yelled from where he was wrestling with one of those huge, horn-sprouting Rhino bastards, "You have wings, bro!"

Furio snorted as newfound powers blazed through him. Fucking hell. It was exactly how Storm and Kingston had both described the extra boost of energy, strength, and magic that had come from just meeting their fated mates.

In the wild, horses had almost three-hundred-sixty-degree vision. He was used to that. But it was what he saw with that vison that made him snort loudly.

Two enormous, diaphanous wings that appeared to be made of fiery green smoke were protruding from his back. Now that was not something he'd ever seen before. He shook his great equine head from side to side but stopped when a scream of pain reached his sensitive ears.

It was her. His mate needed him. Momentary panic at his new wings aside, he crashed across the room and into the bastard who'd been holding her. Stomping him into goo, he lashed out with his back leg and delivered a punishing kick that sent the other Lizard Shifter crashing into what remained of the outer wall of the building. He stomped on that bastard next, growling and snorting in his anger.

"Furio?" Jessenia's voice broke through his murderous anger, and he turned his head to see her smiling at him.

Without delay, he kneeled beside her, grateful when he saw understanding in her amber orbs. Thank fuck. He hardly felt it as she grabbed his mane in her tiny fists and vaulted onto his back.

Furio whinnied as joy flowed through him at having her gentle, reassuring weight resting on him. Heat from her core warmed him and he snorted. His entire body shook with need. He needed to get her home, in his room, in his bed, now.

Turning to see the rest of the Guardians had rounded up those Loyalist assholes, he whinnied once more to get someone's attention. Of course, the Wolf would be the one to turn to him, a wide, knowing grin on the fucker's face.

"Go claim your mate, *cump*," Storm called out, "We got this."

That was all the okay he needed to take off. His heart thundered like thousand revved up engines and when he snorted, he swore he saw the same fiery green smoke his wings were made of stream from his nostrils.

"Take me home," Jessenia's plaintive whisper sped him into action.

Using strength and muscles he didn't even know he had, Furio galloped to the nearest Dragon-made exit. He propelled forward, faster than ever. For a moment, he was scared she'd fall off, but her thighs squeezed him tight. The sound of her laughter peeling out even as she pulled on his mane and hugged his neck close to her chest was exhilarating.

. . .

Fuck, it wasn't just his legs. It was those fiery wings pushing them forward. They were not flying exactly, but he sure as fuck wasn't just running either. This was a speed he'd never achieved before, but he couldn't stop even if he wanted to. Not yet. Not until she was safe.

The cold forest air hit his face like a sharp slap, but he didn't care. The urge to protect his mate, to get her away from danger, was the driving him hard. There was also the primal desire to have her, to mark her as his own once and for all that had him pushing speed limits.

He hardly noticed how far he ran, he just knew he needed to get her away from the bastards who'd chained him before they dared touch his precious female. By the time he slowed down, he saw shadows emerge from the tall pines like long, needlelike spikes across the thick white snow that covered the forest floor.

. . .

Furio halted and whinnied, snorting furiously. Ears back, he used his supernaturally enhanced senses to scout for danger. They were safe. For now. Thank fuck.

"Easy, easy," she leaned forward, and the reassuring pressure of his sweet Jessenia's slight weight on his back caught his attention.

"We're okay," she crooned, "I'm okay now. You did good, *Pony Boy*."

Furio looked around through his Stallion's eyes. Somehow, he'd brought them home to the Keep. Swirls of smoky green magic surrounded him, blinding him. Furio blinked to regain his vision.

One minute he was a Stallion with his mate on his back, the next he was a man, and Jessenia was in his arms. Exactly where she belonged. He recognized that as the only truth he needed.

"We gotta talk about this Pony Boy, nonsense," he said with a grin and arched his brow.

. . .

"Oh yeah," she sassed back, "What about it?"

"I'm not a boy, *piccolina*, I'm a Stallion."

"That might be true," she squinted, "But I am not calling you that in bed."

Heat flashed through their shared humor, and for one moment all he thought was how absolutely crazy he was about her. There was no denying it. No cure for it either. Even if there was, he wouldn't want it.

. . .

She was perfect. Curvy and gorgeous with her soft brown curls and deep eyes that bore into his. Something had shifted between them. Some wonderful and magical thing had changed the atmosphere that existed between the two as they faced off in the chilled February morning.

His chest was heaving with the effort it took not to jump her right then and there. But he knew, oh yes, he knew. She was ready for him to claim her. And he was not going to wait another second.

"Mine," he growled and mashed his mouth to hers.

Chapter Fourteen

"Mine," his voice echoed deep within her, and Jessenia felt the truth of it down to her marrow.

Her tongue swept inside of his mouth, tasting every inch of her magnificent Stallion. She was greedy for him, wanted all of him with every last inch of her.

He must have felt the same. The evidence was long, hot, and hard pressed against her stomach through the fleece she wore.

Fuck, he was naked, she realized. His whole beautiful body was on display, and her powers reacted predictably.

"Mmm," he murmured, refusing to end the kiss

even though she'd zapped him just a tad on his rear end.

What could she say? She'd been waiting months to get her hands on his luscious glutes. But she didn't mean to toast them!

At least, not yet. She tried to pull back, to keep from harming him, but Furio didn't seem willing to end the kiss despite her finicky magic.

"Mine," he growled roughly. The single syllable wreaked havoc on her.

Holy hell. She trembled and went still all at the same time. Jessenia had no idea how he managed to pull that off. All she knew was that the tiny sparks of arousal that had been dancing along her spine had turned into an all-consuming, towering inferno of need.

That and more, she thought, always so much more where he was concerned. Her sex moistened, readying for his invasion, and she moaned in antic-ipation.

"Want you," she admitted against his lips, loving the rumble that seemed to grow inside of him as she finally gave voice to her feelings.

"Bed," he nodded, "now."

With that he lifted her in his arms and those

crazy beautiful, green wings that had magically appeared on his Stallion's form, seemed to wrap around them both, spirting them down the corridor to his room.

By the time he carried her to his door, the thing opened as if by magic. Jessenia smiled around her mouthful of his very clever tongue. The Keep approved, or so it would seem, she thought.

The magical manse was known for tending to its Guardians and their mates' every need. And she needed this, wanted it with every bit of her. Finally, she was going to lay claim to her Stallion.

"Mine," he breathed the word, laying her out on the bed like something prized and precious.

Her face flamed, but she pushed her embarrassment away. This was Furio. Her Furio. She bit her lip, and he peeled away the layers of clothing she'd worn to protect herself against the cold. She'd done things in the last few days she would have never imagined herself capable of.

He gave her the strength to see it through, she thought with wonder. His belief in her was everything. Hell, she rushed into battle and fought to get him back.

As if sensing her thoughts, Furio cupped her cheeks and kissed her forehead, her cheeks, her chin, and her mouth. Softly though. Gently, too. And not nearly long enough, she thought greedily, even as he pressed his forehead to hers.

"Thank you," he said in a voice rough with emotion, "for coming to get me, but you have to promise to never do that again."

"No," she shook her head and tugged his head back down to hers when he tried to move away, "I won't promise that. I will always come for you, Furio."

"Jess," he shook his head, eyes glittering down at her.

"Always. If I am yours, then that makes you mine too," she stated baldly, "Now, are you going to claim me, or what?"

The taunt was just enough to push him over the edge. Furio growled as the thin hold he had over his self-control snapped.

"Yes," she moaned as her Stallion took the neck-line of her sweater, the only article of clothing left on her body, and tore the thing off her.

He stood up between her splayed legs that were hanging off his bed, appraising her with his glittering green eyes. She watched, breathlessly as his gaze seemed to devour her.

Jessenia was not an exhibitionist. Short and

curvy, she'd been the nerdy girl in high school. The one who clung to her comfortable sweats and flannels, hiding her chubby body from the mean girls and judgmental jocks.

Fergie was her only real friend from her childhood, and though she was also a curvy girl, the woman owned that shit. But Jessenia wasn't a dorky teenager anymore, and she'd learned to be comfortable in her own skin.

Even so, no one had ever looked at her quite like that. Her pussy grew wetter under his steady green stare. She loved his eyes, loved them on her. Her breast swelled, nipples hardened, all in preparation for him. Only him.

Sex had never been like this. No, this was magic at its best, she thought as her powers reflexively reached out to stroke his skin. She felt it inside of her, as if she was touching him with her hands. His eyes widened, and he growled, leaning into the ethereal touch and licking his plump lips.

Jessenia followed the move with her eyes, desperate to do so with her tongue. Her breath came in short, quick bursts, but Furio shook his head. He wasn't budging until he'd looked his fill.

She could neither talk nor could she look away.

Everything was contingent on his next move. It seemed like eons passed, but it was more like seconds until those limitless green pools met her searching stare.

"Ah, *piccolina*, you are so beautiful," he said, and reached out with trembling hands to touch her, "So perfect."

Jessenia closed her eyes and allowed herself to simply feel as he learned her body with his deliciously rough, callused fingers. His fingertips grazed her hair, cheeks, her lips, the slope of her neck until they rested on her chest above where she wanted him so badly.

"What is it, *piccolina?*"

"Touch me," she begged, unashamed as her hips flexed of their own accord, and her back arched, searching for more from him.

"I am touching you," he leaned on the bed, continuing the slow steady stroke of his hands across her clavicle.

"More, Furio, please," she arched again, gasping as he traced her nipples with light feathery, barely there touches.

"Like this?" he asked.

Jessenia shook her head. Eyes closed, she whimpered in need. He was driving her nuts, but when she reached out to take control, he clamped his other hand around her wrists and held them against the mattress above her head.

"Uh uh," he grunted, "I have been waiting months to touch you, *piccolina*. It's my turn."

"Then do it," she said, frustration making her angry, "Touch me, and stop fucking around."

"It's never fucking around with you," he grinned and finally, cupped one hand around her aching bud, "Your breasts are gorgeous," he growled over her harsh moan.

"They're small," she answered and moaned as he skimmed his heated palms over each hardened nubbin.

He growled and lightened his touches, carefully molding the soft, plump flesh of her breasts, and she whimpered at the loss of friction. For a bigger woman, her breasts were decidedly average-sized. She'd often wondered if that was a blessing or curse, but the way he was petting them and praising her, she had to believe the former.

"They're perfect," he corrected, bending his head to take one inside his hot mouth, "I love your pink, dusky nipples," he sucked her hard, then released her bud with a soft pop, "Love the way they feel and taste in my mouth."

He growled and bent his head again, suckling one breast then the other. She writhed beneath his attentions. Gasping as the pleasure heightened, and not-so-secretly reveling in the fact that no matter what, he did not let up. Not for a minute.

She felt moisture pool between her legs, and her pussy throbbed. Empty. Needy. Fuck, she wanted him so bad. Never like this, she thought.

Her mouth opened, and she whimpered against the constant pressure of his mouth on her sensitive nipples. The tugging sensation sent waves of pleasure rolling through her. She was slick and ready for him, but he took his time.

Damn him, she winced as his teeth grazed her nipple causing her to hiss.

Love him, her magic corrected.

Fine. She loved him. And she wanted to show him. Tugging on his hold, she whimpered when he let go of her wrists. Still, Furio was not about to be rushed. She tugged on his head, but he just growled and licked and tasted her skin, whispering all the things he was going to do to her between his hot kisses.

"Furio," she tugged on his hair as he hovered over her, attempting to push him where she wanted him most.

"So impatient," he grinned at her.

"Please."

"Don't worry, *piccolina*, I have everything you need."

Her desire was almost painful now. Spreading her legs wide as he slid down her body, Jessenia flexed her hips, rubbing her mound on his hardened abs.

The friction made her hiss, and he growled in response. The sexy sound reverberated through to her soul, and she gasped.

Furio used his long, slick tongue to lick his way down her chest, giving one last tug on each nipple before sliding further down. She cringed slightly as he reached her soft belly, her arms reflexively moving to cover herself, but he would have none of that.

"Mine," his voice had somehow gotten even deeper, and she whimpered in need, "never hide from me, baby. You are beautiful, perfect. Made for me."

"Yes," she nodded, accepting his words as truth.

Her magic pulsed, as if agreeing with him. She'd

learned the hard way to trust her powers, and she didn't want to make the same mistakes here.

Jessenia knew she belonged with him. He was hers as much as she was his. If he said he wanted her the way she was, then he did. And the result of that knowledge was instantaneous. A wave of heat flooded her, her pussy clenching on air, needy for him.

"Need you," she moaned.

Honesty was like breathing to the Guardians, as far as she could tell. She knew Shifters could scent lies, so most of them avoided it, but it was not the same with Witches. They could lie, hell they had to. For centuries, lying about their magic kept them alive. But there would be no lies between them. Not even ones of omission. Not anymore.

"Gonna give you what you need. First, I gotta taste you, mate," he slid down further, nipping her hip with his blunt-edged teeth.

Furio's rough hands found her thighs, pushing her legs open even wider. He teased the sensitive flesh with his fingertips. Tracing circles up her thighs till he was parting her outer lips.

Her body was so aroused, even that tiny flitting gesture had her moaning. She gasped at the sensations that rushed through her as she leaned on her elbows and watched him stare at her needy sex.

"Furio," she whined his name, flexing her hips to entice him closer.

Okay, so she was a total slut for the man. She couldn't help it. Her whole body was wound tight. Like she'd been waiting for his touch for an eternity. Maybe she had.

"Ah, *piccolina*, you smell so fucking good. Gonna taste even better," he growled, and finally, his oh-so-flexible and talented lips found her core.

Holy shit. Jessenia's gasp echoed in the room. Was that a Horse thing? She could only wonder as he buried his face between her legs. His thick fingers dug into her thighs as he expertly nibbled her sensitive flesh, and she wanted them buried deep inside her.

But she was not content to be idle. No, she was no bystander. Fuck that. Jessenia swiveled her hips, grinding her pussy into his face. She moaned aloud when he finally pressed one thick digit into her sopping wet heat.

Thank fuck, she thought, as he began to move. Curling his finger and stroking in short, upwards motions, he found that perfect spot deep inside that incited a husky, deep moan to eke out from her parted lips.

"More," she begged, and he gave it to her.

Adding another finger as his tongue curled around her clit in times with his deep strokes. More heat pooled as his fingers still caressed her walls. All the while, Furio continued to lick and nibble her sensitive nubbin until she thought she was going to explode.

Jessenia wound her hands through his long, thick locks. Holding him where she wanted him, she rocked her hips, chasing her pleasure.

"Come for me," Furio commanded, then he sucked on the tiny swollen nub. *Hard.*

Jessenia's mouth opened wide, and she yelled as she rode his hand and mouth. Explosions of pleasure went off, starting inside and working their way throughout her entire body.

Wave after wave of ecstasy flowed through her. She threw her head back and yelled his name, claiming the utter joy he'd gifted her in this, their shared passion.

"Mine," she said, tugging his hair until he moved up her body, so their faces were close together.

Then she kissed him. Tasting herself on his lips,

Jessenia moaned around his tongue as her hands smoothed over his muscled back until she reached his ass. She continued to pet and stroke him until she found his thick cock, placing his head at her soaked entrance.

"Make me yours," she said, noting the fire in his emerald gaze.

"Mine," he growled and pushed deep inside.

Finally.

Chapter Fifteen

Furio was in heaven. There was no other way to describe the absolute bliss of finally sinking into his mate's tight, hot body. Months of banked down desire came rushing forward as he pressed deeper.

Careful to make sure he did not hurt his *piccolina*, he couldn't stop until every inch of his cock was buried deep inside her slick pussy.

Sweet unobliterated heaven, he thought again, growling her name between tight lips.

"Jessenia. Mine."

Mate, he grunted and settled his big body between her splayed thighs. She was so small, so perfect. Her tight sheath stretched around him, caressing him like a velvet vise. Her body cradled his, so soft and warm, the perfect foil for his hardness.

She was his now, and he was never letting go. She had to know that. Once she allowed him, *him* with all his faults and rough edges, to sink into her, that was it.

"Mate," he said against her mouth, before claiming her lips.

He pulled out slowly, then pushed in again, groaning in pleasure as he buried himself to the hilt. Giving her a moment to adjust to his length and girth, he hissed when his *piccolina* wiggled impatiently. Drawing a smile from his lips, even as he refused to give hers up.

No way. He had every intention of continuing to claim those plump, pink lips of hers. Furio wanted to kiss her, and kiss her, and keep on kissing her until he was drunk with it. After months of denying himself, he couldn't seem to stop.

"Don't stop then," she returned, "I want to kiss you too."

Her tongue tangled with his, and he felt the pleasure she felt when she was kissing him back. It made his soul sing with joy. He wasn't sure if he'd spoken aloud, or if she'd simply read his mind. It didn't matter. He wasn't going to stop. Not until they were both too boneless to move.

Being inside Jessenia was like every dream he'd had in the months since he'd met her coming true all at once. She was so beautiful and so fucking responsive.

Her body was more than welcoming. Every plunge and withdrawal, flex and swivel was in time with his. Every time he pushed his cock deep, he felt her channel tighten and stroke him perfectly.

She lifted her hips to meet his with just the right amount of pressure, the perfect pace. Like she was made for him.

Yes, he supposed, she was made for him. His one true and fated mate. His perfect match in every way. And fuck it, he could admit it now. He loved her. Would show her how he felt now with his body. And he did.

Arching his back, he swiveled his hips, grinding his pubis into her as she moaned his name. Her nails scored his back as she lifted to meet his thrusts. Every nerve ending aflame, Furio damn near burst apart as joy and wonder filled him.

He reached between them with his hand, tapping her clit in time with his thrusts. Her pussy tightened, and his balls drew close to his body with the need to come.

"Come for me," he growled, mashing his lips to hers before sliding down to her neck.

"Furio," she ground out his name, caught in a soundless scream, her back arched.

He opened his mouth and sucked on that sensitive spot just under her ear that he noticed earlier. Faster and harder, he made love to his sweet mate.

Thrust, withdraw, thrust, swivel, swivel, grind, tap, tap, tap. His own need to come, the desire to fill her with his seed was damn near overwhelming. He wanted her bearing his mate mark. Wanted her to belong to him in every way. And she would. As soon as she came.

He worked harder. Had to. His Stallion whinnied. The beast wanted him to claim her already, but he wouldn't, not until he brought her to orgasm. The Stallion snorted at him, demanding he get on with it already.

Fucking hell. He couldn't think. Her sweet, hot body was molded to his. Furio was never so fucking grateful in his entire life. Jessenia was in his bed, with him, and as he sank balls deep into her honeyed pussy over and over again.

"Perfect, mate," he praised his *piccolina*, thanking the heavens she'd chosen him.

"Close," she moaned, and his balls tightened again with the need to explode.

Her words seemed to pull something loose. Whatever restraint he'd been holding onto, and he roared with need. Lifting her legs to his shoulders until she was practically bent in half.

"Come, *piccolina*. Gonna claim you, but you gotta come for me. That's good," he growled as her sex squeezed him tighter, "S'very good."

Thank fuck. He felt her walls tighten as he increased his tempo. Hands gripping her thighs, lips locked around her neck, Furio's movements took on a wild, positively feral pace.

Passion built, straining, bulging, threatening to drown him, until finally she screamed his name. Arching beneath him, mouth open as her sex continued to squeeze and suck his cock, milking him for all he was worth, Furio opened his mouth and bit down.

A Stallion's bite differed from that of other Shifters. He knew he had to be careful. Without fangs to cut and sink into her skin, his mark would be created by far more blunted incisors that would essentially pinch rather than slice through her skin.

Powerful, but painful if not done correctly. And he would never want to hurt her, which is why timing was key.

Furio's orgasm rushed forward as hers reached its pinnacle. Without delay, he bit down on her skin, marking and claiming her as his own for all time.

Bodies straining against each other, slick with sex and sweat. He roared against her throat as her pussy continued to grip and squeeze him. He filled her with his seed, marking her with his cum as surely as he marked her with his bite.

Heaven, he thought again. She was heaven in his arms.

"Mine," he grunted when they were nothing more than a sweaty tangle of limbs.

"I love you," she said. Her small hands reached up to cup his face, and she lifted her sweet mouth to his.

"I love you too, *piccolina*," he smiled through the tears that pricked his eyes.

Rolling over until she was astride his hips, Furio gripped her thick thighs.

"Love you so much," he growled, kissing her lips, loving how her eyes went all amber and wide once she realized his cock was hard again, and still buried inside her sheath.

"Can you?"

"I'm a Shifter," he said and lifted her hips.

"You're a Stallion," she corrected, taking the reins and slamming her body back down on his shaft.

"I'm your Stallion," he said.

"Good, cause I want to ride," she moaned into his mouth, pushing on his chest until he lay flat beneath her.

Fuck, she was glorious. Her curly hair hung in wild disarray as she continued to make love to him. And it was loving. Always would be.

"Mate," he reached for her, and together they made it to heights he'd never imagined.

Through it all, Furio kissed her. He was still kissing her, hours later when they'd managed to make love across his room from the bed, to the floor, the sofa, his gaming chair, and the brand-new loft he'd been working on with the Keep just for her.

"I can't believe you built this for me," she said from her position on top of him, which was quickly becoming his favorite if he did say so himself.

"I love you," he shrugged, "want you happy."

"You make me happy," she grinned, "This is just cake."

"Speaking of cake," he said, and she groaned.

"I knew you just wanted me for my carrot cake,"

she started, then collapsed in a fit of giggles under his tickle-assault tactics.

"No, baby, I wanted you for this," he dropped his head and kissed her again.

"Mm," she sighed, "I love you, but if you want to do this again, I need food."

"Food? Why didn't you say so?"

He pulled her up and carried her to the shower. Yes, he was more than pleased to find she liked the skylight and mini greenhouse he'd built on the new loft in his, *now their*, bedroom. He wanted to show her how happy he was, but first, she needed feeding.

Epilogue

"He built you a loft?"

"Yep," Jessenia was positively glowing.

She could feel happiness radiating from her pores. Yes, he'd bult her a loft in his room complete with an enormous skylight and row upon row of shelves for her herbs and organic lettuce.

Cooking was her passion, but both her edible recipes and her Witchy ones required fresh ingredients. The outdoor greenhouse would be a wonderful addition, undoubtedly. But this was her own bit of heaven.

Well, besides being with him. She sighed and ignored the gagging sounds coming from her best friend.

"So, you know you are sick, right? Getting hot and bothered over some shelves for your plants?"

"For my herbs, but anyway," she answered Fergie while she prepared a midnight snack for her and her mate, which included a fresh carrot cake for her lover, "you should talk. I heard you and Storm banging against the wall after your latest shoe delivery arrived last week."

"What? Do you know how long I've been waiting for those slouchy *Manolo Blahnik* suede boots to come in red and in my size?" she blew a raspberry at Jessenia, who laughed and rolled her eyes while she added a handful of pignoli nuts to her pesto.

Thank goodness, the Keep had a way with the gas range and ovens. *A magical way.*

She'd no more than tossed ingredients together than the ovens magicked them ready. Dessert was iced and on the tray. The pasta was finished, and she was just waiting on the garlic bread.

"Holy crap! I admit that smells better than my sandwiches, but me and my boo need the meats," Fergie sniffed and frowned, "So, you are going vegetarian, huh?"

"Not really," Jessenia shrugged, "I just wanted pasta."

She hadn't thought about it, but the idea of not eating meat wasn't exactly repulsive. Either way, she knew Furio had no preference. He just wanted her happy. And wasn't that awesome?

Sappy sigh.

"You know, Jess, I wanted you to know I was chatting with everyone tonight and, well, they all love Furio here. No one is mad at him, least of all Holley."

Fergie reached out and took Jessenia's hand. Tugging the woman in for a hug, she wiped her eyes and smiled.

"Good," she said, "Because he loves all of you too. We both do."

"Good," Fergie cleared her throat, "Families fight, and you're both our family. You know that, right?"

Jessenia's heart damn near burst, but she just nodded. Both women hastily wiped their faces. After years of knowing each other, making bald statements like that were cause for a little emotion. She wasn't uncomfortable with it, but it would definitely keep.

"You ready?" Storm came into the kitchen and took the tray of ham sandwiches Fergie had grabbed from the fridge for the two of them, "Wassup Jess?"

"Hey," she smiled, looking behind him for her mate, "Where is Furio?"

Two arms wrapped around her from behind, and her pulse sped up. She recognized him immediately by scent, touch, and the pulsing matebond that connected them. Sighing happily, she returned his embrace. Loving how he always wanted to snuggle and touch her. Needing that connection herself.

"Mate," he whispered and kissed the spot on her neck that bore her mark.

She shivered in response. That spot would always be a source of arousal and pleasure for her. She somehow knew that, just like she knew how much he truly loved her. It was something to do with their matebond, she realized.

As a Witch, he'd managed to convince her to drop the whole kitchen thing since her powers were proving more badassed by the minute. She understood the matebond they shared was deeply steeped in magic.

Even so, she'd never have imagined such a powerful connection with another being. But Furio truly was made just for her.

"How's Kingston and Holley?" she asked him, knowing full well where he'd gone while she insisted on preparing a meal for them.

"Good," he said, "The tea helped, and he said to tell you the healer wants to talk to you, but I told him in the morning."

"Okay," she nodded, "I can do that tomorrow. I want to check in on her, anyway."

She was so thankful the other Witch had been looked at by an ancient healer, and that her tea had helped. But she was also glad they would have the rest of the night alone.

"Hey yo, cump," Storm nodded at her mate, "We sparring in the morning?"

"You know it," Furio answered, and she could tell he was happy.

Life at the Keep was definitely moving forward. And that was a good thing. They all needed that. The Keep and the Guardians and mates who dwelled there were connected in a way that most people would never understand. Jessenia's heart swelled with pride and feeling when she thought that she was officially a part of that now. Because of him. Her mate.

"Catch you two later," Fergie giggled after Storm whispered in her ear.

They waved their farewells and took off down the hall.

"Come on," Furio took the covered tray from her hands, and together they walked to their bedroom.

"So, I smell pasta," he grinned, trying to guess what she'd made them.

"Yep, pesto," she returned knowing full well it was his favorite, "and for dessert."

"Carrot cake?" he looked so dang hopeful.

"Yes," she cleared her throat.

"I don't need carrot cake, *piccolina*, or pesto, or anything else. You know that, right?"

"I know," she grinned, "I just like cooking."

"And you are great at it, but I love you for so much more than that," Furio placed the tray on the small table in front of the sofa by the television.

Grabbing her hips, he pulled her flush against him, and pressed his forehead to hers. She loved it when he did that. It was like he just wanted to breathe her in, to be still for a moment in a world that was sometimes too crazy and loud, moving too fast to understand. But this here, with him, this was her anchor. He was her strength, her hearth, her home.

"Mate," she whispered the word.

Testing it on her lips, she liked how it felt, but it was too important not to simply shout it. She did not want to break the peace of the moment or the magic she'd felt being with him.

"Hearing you say that does things to me," he confessed, "You have no idea. You are everything to me, *piccolina*," his voice was rough, and she opened her eyes to see his glittering down at her.

"Are you sure?" she asked, finally giving voice to her greatest fear.

"Oh Jess, I choose you, always. Willingly, willfully, fated mate or not, you are the only one I want. Forever. Mine," he cupped her face in his hands, and pressed his hard body against hers.

Then he bent down and took her mouth in a kiss that pushed away any lingering doubts she'd had. This was as real as it got.

Furio was her Stallion. Her mate. Her shield against harm, now and forever. Food forgotten, they tore clothes off each other in their need to connect.

Joy and pure bliss pulsed through their mate-bond, and Jessenia moaned with happiness as he entered her in one, perfectly executed thrust. Coming together with him was a soul-deep connection she craved, like oxygen.

When she was with him, everything else fell away. He was her love, her life, and she was so ready to embrace that. To be his mate in every way.

When they were finally spent, hours later, Furio nuzzled her neck, kissed her mate mark, and together they slept wrapped in the warmth of the bed they'd made and unmade together. And they would do it again tomorrow, and all the other tomorrows they got on this Earth together.

"I love you," she said.

"I love you too," he affirmed, "Always, *piccolina*."

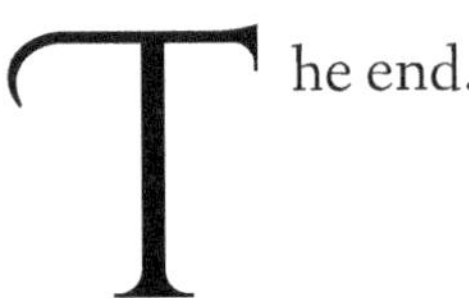

The end.

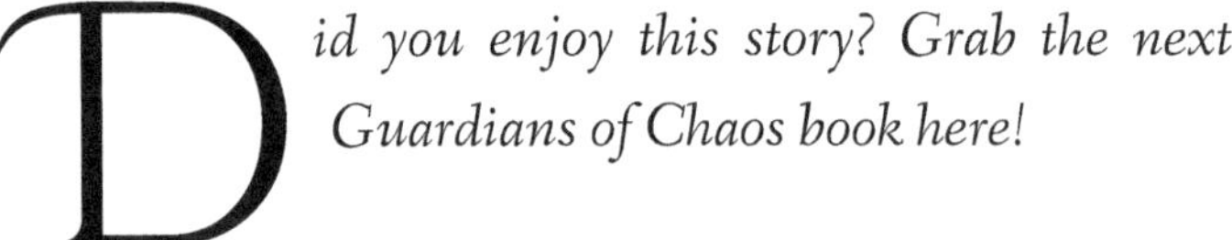

Did you enjoy this story? Grab the next Guardians of Chaos book here!

P.S

Don't forget to tell me how you liked this story by leaving your honest review! *No pressure.* 😉

A review can be one or two brief sentences where you simply state whether you enjoyed the story and would recommend it to someone! It is an enormous help to authors and the best way for us to reach larger audiences so we can keep writing the stories you love!

Thank you so much!

Xoxo!

Del mare alla stella,

C.D. Gorri

Have you met my Dragons?

The Falk Clan Tales are my stories surrounding four Dragon Shifter brothers and how they find their one true mates.

Each brother's chest is marked with his rose, the magical link to his heart and his magic. They each have a matching gemstone to go with it.

She's given up on love, but he's just begun.

In *The Dragon's Valentine* we meet the eldest Falk brother, Callius. He is on a mission to find a Castle and his one true mate, one he can trust with his diamond rose....

His heart is frozen; can she change his mind about love?

In *The Dragon's Christmas Gift* our attention shifts to Alexsander, the youngest brother of the four. He has resigned himself to a life alone, until he meets *her*.

Some wounds run deep, can a Dragon's heart be unbroken?

The Dragon's Heart is the story of Edric Falk who has vowed never to love again, but that changes when he meets his feisty mate, Joselyn Curacao.

She just wants a little fun, he's looking for a lifetime.

We finally meet Nikolai Falk and his sexy Shifter mate in *The Dragon's Secret*.

Now available in a boxed set.

Look for The Dragon's Treasure in 2022!

Connect with C.D. Gorri

To learn more about me please visit:

https://www.cdgorri.com

https://www.facebook.com/Cdgorribooks

https://twitter.com/cgor22

https://www.bookbub.com/authors/c-d-gorri

TikTok

Visit my website to find out more about my supernatural world also known as the Grazi Kelly Universe and sign up to be a subscriber!

https://www.cdgorri.com/newsletter

Have you met my Bears?

Looking for a Paranormal Romance series that is loads of growly fun?

Meet the Barvale Clan first in the Bear Claw Tales! A complete shifter romance series about 4 brothers who discover and need to win their fated mates!

Followed by two more spin off series, the Barvale Clan Tales and the Barvale Holiday Tales!

No cliffhangers. Steamy PNR fun. Go and read your next happily ever after today!

Other Titles by C.D. Gorri

Other Titles by C.D. Gorri

Young Adult Urban Fantasy Books:

Wolf Moon: A Grazi Kelly Novel Book 1

Hunter Moon: A Grazi Kelly Novel Book 2

Rebel Moon: A Grazi Kelly Novel Book 3

Winter Moon: A Grazi Kelly Novel Book 4

Chasing The Moon: A Grazi Kelly Short 5

Blood Moon: A Grazi Kelly Novel 6

*Get all 6 books NOW AVAILABLE IN A BOXED SET:

The Complete Grazi Kelly Novel Series

Casting Magic: The Angela Tanner Files 1

Keeping Magic: The Angela Tanner Files 2

G'Witches Magical Mysteries Series

Co-written with P. Mattern

G'Witches

G'Witches 2: The Hary Harbinger

Paranormal Romance Books:

Macconwood Pack Novel Series:

Charley's Christmas Wolf: A Macconwood Pack Novel 1

Cat's Howl: A Macconwood Pack Novel 2

Code Wolf: A Macconwood Pack Novel 3

The Witch and The Werewolf: A Macconwood Pack Novel 4

To Claim a Wolf: A Macconwood Pack Novel 5

Conall's Mate: A Macconwood Pack Novel 6

Her Solstice Wolf: A Macconwood Pack Novel 7

Also available in 2 boxed sets:

The Macconwood Pack Volume 1

The Macconwood Pack Volume 2

Macconwood Pack Tales Series:

Wolf Bride: The Story of Ailis and Eoghan A Macconwood Pack Tale 1

Summer Bite: A Macconwood Pack Tale 2

His Winter Mate: A Macconwood Pack Tale 3

Snow Angel: A Macconwood Pack Tale 4

Charley's Baby Surprise: A Macconwood Pack Tale 5

Home for the Howlidays: A Macconwood Pack Tale 6

A Silver Wedding: A Macconwood Pack Tale 7

Mine Furever: A Macconwood Pack Tale 8

A Furry Little Christmas: A Macconwood Pack Tale 9

Also available in two boxed sets:

The Macconwood Pack Tales Volume 1

Shifters Furever: The Macconwood Pack Tales Volume 2

The Falk Clan Tales:

The Dragon's Valentine: A Falk Clan Novel 1

The Dragon's Christmas Gift: A Falk Clan Novel 2

The Dragon's Heart: A Falk Clan Novel 3

The Dragon's Secret: A Falk Clan Novel 4

The Dragon's Treasure: A Falk Clan Novel 5

Dragon Mates: The Falk Clan Complete Series Boxed Set Books 1-4

The Bear Claw Tales:

Bearly Breathing: A Bear Claw Tale 1

Bearly There: A Bear Claw Tale 2

Bearly Tamed: A Bear Claw Tale 3

Bearly Mated: A Bear Claw Tale 4

Also available in a boxed set:

The Complete Bear Claw Tales (Books 1-4)

<u>The Barvale Clan Tales:</u>

Polar Opposites: The Barvale Clan Tales 1

Polar Outbreak: The Barvale Clan Tales 2

Polar Compound: A Barvale Clan Tale 3

Polar Curve: A Barvale Clan Tale 4

<u>Barvale Holiday Tales:</u>

A Bear For Christmas

Hers To Bear

Thank You Beary Much

<u>Purely Paranormal Pleasures:</u>

Marked by the Devil: Purely Paranormal Pleasures

Mated to the Dragon King: Purely Paranormal Pleasures

Claimed by the Demon: Purely Paranormal Pleasures

Christmas with a Devil, a Dragon King, & a Demon: Purely Paranormal Pleasures (short story)

Vampire Lover: Purely Paranormal Pleasures

Grizzly Lover: Purely Paranormal Pleasures

Elvish Lover: Purely Paranormal Pleasures

Hot Dire Wolf Nights: Purely Paranormal Pleasures

Christmas With Her Chupacabra: Purely Paranormal Pleasures

<u>The Wardens of Terra:</u>

Bound by Air: The Wardens of Terra Book 1

Star Kissed: A Wardens of Terra Short

Waterlocked: The Wardens of Terra Book 2

Moon Kissed: A Wardens of Terra Short

*Now in a boxed set and in audio!

The Maverick Pride Tales:

Purrfectly Mated: Paranormal Dating Agency: A Maverick Pride Tale 1

Purrfectly Kissed: Paranormal Dating Agency: A Maverick Pride Tale 2

Purrfectly Trapped: Paranormal Dating Agency: A Maverick Pride Tale 3

Purrfectly Caught: Paranormal Dating Agency: A Maverick Pride Tale 4

Purrfectly Naughty: Paranormal Dating Agency: A Maverick Pride Tale 5

Purrfectly Bound: Paranormal Dating Agency: A Maverick Pride Tale 6

Also available in 2 boxed sets:

The Maverick Pride Volume 1

The Maverick Pride Volume 2

Dire Wolf Mates:

Shake That Sass: Sassy Ever After: Dire Wolf Mates Book 1

Breaking Sass: Sassy Ever After: Dire Wolf Mates 2

Pinch of Sass: Sassy Ever After: Dire Wolf Mates 3

Also available in a boxed set:

Dire Wolf Mates Volume 1

Wyvern Protection Unit:

Trusting Her Protector

Tempting Her Protector

Tricking Her Protector

Standalones:

The Enforcer

Blood Song: A Sanguinem Council Book

EveL Worlds:

Chinchilla and the Devil: A FUCN'A BookSammi and the
Jersey Bull: A FUCN'A Book

The Guardians of Chaos:

Wolf Shield: Guardians of Chaos Book 1

Dragon Shield: Guardians of Chaos Book 2

Stallion Shield: Guardians of Chaos Book 3

Panther Shield: Guardians of Chaos 4

Howl's Romance

Mated to the Werewolf Next Door: A Howl's Romance

The Tiger King's Christmas Bride

Claiming His Virgin Mate: Howls Romance

Twice Mated Tales

Doubly Claimed

Doubly Bound

Doubly Tied

Hearts of Stone Series

Shifter Mountain: Hearts of Stone 1

Shifter City: Hearts of Stone 2

Accidentally Undead Series

Fangs For Nothin'

Moongate Island Tales

Moongate Island Mate

Mated in Hope Falls

Mated by Moonlight

Shifters Unleashed Boxed Sets

Check out these amazing anthologies where you can find some of my books

and the works of other awesome authors!

Coming Soon:

Ash: Speed Dating with the Denizens of Hell

Hungry Like Her Wolf: Magic and Mayhem Universe

Shifter Village: Hearts of Stone 3

Midnight Magic Anthology (Water Witch)

Mouse and the Ball: A FUCN'A Book

Tiger Claimed

For Fangs Sake

Tiger Denied

Werewolf Fever: A Macconwood Pack Novel 8

Moongate Island Captive

Witch Shield: Guardians of Chaos 5

Sweet As Candy (as seen in Once Upon An Ever After)

Taming Magic: The Angela Tanner Files 3

Rituals & Runes Anthology (Air Witch)

Excerpt from Code Wolf

"Are you fuckin' with me?"

"No, Randall, I assure you I am not fuckin' with you," Rafe Maccon eased his immense frame back into his oversized, black leather chair and narrowed his ice blue eyes at his Third and one of his oldest friends. How long had he known the man sitting in front of him?

Randall had come to Maccon City when Rafe was about ten, he looked the same then as he did now. Tall at six foot three inches, muscular, and more than a little intimidating to the Wolves under him with his long beard and equally long dark brown hair.

Rafe, however, was the Alpha. He was more amused than intimidated by his surly friend.

"A vacation?! What the fuck am I gonna do on a vacation? Come on, Rafe, this is bullshit!"

The door to Rafe's private office flew open and in strolled a very happy, very pregnant Charley Maccon, Rafe's wife. The Alpha's eyes glowed as they landed on his positively glowing mate. She wore a long, flowy dress. The shade was a pale-yellow color that, Randall admitted to himself, looked damn good with her creamy complexion and curly dark hair.

Their Alpha Female was quite something. There wasn't a Wolf Guard in the place who wouldn't lay down his/her life for her.

"Well, maybe you should consider a vacation to be a relaxing experience, Randy," she dropped a kiss on Randall's cheek and walked past him, over to her husband whom she kissed full on the mouth.

The way his Alpha's eyes homed in on her when she opened the door was nothing compared to the hungry gaze that followed her across the room.

Randall had noticed it took a while for Rafe to get used to his mate's habit of greeting everyone with a kiss or hug. Wolves were protective of their mates, but Randall thought his Alpha was doing an exceedingly good job of hiding his tension. Werewolves did not share very well.

Charley; however, had stood firm. That was the way she was raised, and she wasn't going to change for any, how had she put it? Neanderthal browbeating husband, regardless of how cute his ass was!

Randall had no direct knowledge if the "cute ass" statement was true or not. And he didn't want to know. He liked Charley though, had from the beginning. He was musically inclined and often took to one of the common rooms to strum his guitar or play a few keys on the piano.

Excerpt from Shifter Mountain
by C.D. Gorri

Keeton's Mountain Lion hissed angrily as he boarded the plane for the States. Three months on Moongate Island did nothing to repair his faith in people. Shifter or human, they pretty much sucked.

True, he was no longer being blackmailed by the sniveling cretin who'd been part of his last black ops assignment. Fucker had stepped on a landmine deep in the jungles of a place Keeton was not at liberty to name. Not even in his own head.

Fucking hell.

Yeah, it meant he could return home now, but to who? Keeton had no family waiting for him. His few friends were back on the island, but that was no place for his inner feline. The beast craved the hills and valleys of the New Jersey forests he called home.

He'd bought a hundred acres of forest off the beaten paths of New Jersey's Panther Mountains years ago. Even commissioned the building of a cabin deep in the woods. The design was environmentally conscientious and entirely sound. Two stories high, it had its own generators, additional solar paneling, and wind turbines for power, and indoor plumbing.

He wasn't an animal, for fuck's sake. But even if Keeton was going to avoid people, he didn't have to be uncomfortable doing it. Eyes closed, he sat seemingly at ease, but he was keeping tabs on every living thing around him on the plane.

Once a soldier, always a soldier, his two commanders, Callan McGregor and Landry Smyth, had said that often enough. Both men were Shifters, a unique Alpha and Omega pair who'd completed their Triad once they'd found their mate in Sage Freeman, a smart mouthed human female. That had been Keeton's cue to leave the island he'd called home for eighty-nine and a half days.

They hadn't kicked him out or anything. On the contrary. But he was restless and antsy. The island could no longer contain his need for isolation.

Memories of the disgust on Bruce Taylor's face when he'd seen Keeton lose control of his shift during a particularly bloody battle were forever ingrained in his brain. The human male had been a new recruit in the special ops task force where Keeton had served his country for the last five years in secret.

Dismantling dictatorships and stopping atrocities the likes of which he could hardly put a name to before they could ever see the light of day had been his job, and blackmail was his reward.

He'd kept the fact that he'd unwittingly told the secret about Shifters to the human from Callan and Landry until the night Bruce had died believing Keeton was the only one of his kind. The two men had investigated his claims, making sure that he never downloaded or emailed the proof he'd recorded with his phone the night Keeton lost control.

The half a million dollars he'd sent to Bruce's offshore bank was nothing. He didn't care about the money. It was simply the point of it all. The man had not trusted Keeton because of his dual nature. And he'd lost his life as a result.

"We need to stick to this route, Bruce," he growled *at the human who'd become increasingly toxic to their two-man operation.*

"Think I'm gonna trust a fucking animal. I'll go this way," the man argued.

After a few more minutes of trying to convince him, Keeton threw his hands up. His beast scratched at his skin, the animal sensing something was not right. The sounds of the explosion and Bruce's bitter cry rang in his ears, but he died before Keeton could ever hope to reach him.

It was his fault. He was the reason Bruce had died. After pledging his life to help save lives, he'd brought death instead.

Keeton was better off on his own.

Excerpt from Fangs For Nothin'
by C.D. Gorri

"Are you out of your mind?"

Xavier DuMont, Vampire and Prince of the Tenebris Clan out of DuMont, New Jersey, ran a hand over his face. It was almost five in the morning on Wednesday, and he was still going over the weekly requests and complaints.

He could not believe it. One after the other, he'd received dozens of requests for formal introductions for most of the eligible young females in the Clan by their parents or some family matchmaker or other. It was the 21st Century, and yet, the Vampires of the Tenebris Clan still thought he needed an arranged marriage to run things!

"No, Lucius, I assure you my mind is sound."

"How can you be thinking of going away? To some retreat? At this time of year! You know, the whole Clan is up in arms over the tax laws your father had set into motion before his demise. Some are questioning your right to rule. Then, there is still the matter of your mating—"

"Lucius, for the love of fuck! I know what is going on in my own Clan. I am even now revoking those tax laws, people will just have to be patient."

"And what about meeting with these young females? Maybe that will quell some of the unrest—"

"No! I am not inclined to take a mate at this time. My father's grave has barely begun to grow grass. There is no rush!"

"There is pressure though, sire," Lucius Redwing insisted.

He was Xavier's oldest and most reliable friend. At nearly three hundred years old, they'd known each other for a considerable length of time. Lucius had been his childhood companion when they'd fled France for the New World. After settling the town of DuMont, his father had not only been the most productive of the local normals, but he had taken over their branch of the Clan.

Breaking ties with the old regime, and establishing their own rule, the DuMonts had done exceedingly well. Of course, coming into the new century had been difficult for some, but Xavier was determined to do it, to breathe new life into the old-fashioned world of Vampires. He would see them succeed and blossom in this age that was simply exploding with technology.

"I know you have plans, sire. But the anxious mamas are already parading their daughters resumes as if they were applying for a job." Lucius grinned. He waved a manila envelope bursting with applications for audiences with him from the most prestigious Vampire families in all of DuMont.

"For fuck's sake, Luc. Get rid of them," Xavier growled, and ran a hand over his face.

"Now, now. Surely, you know enough not to disrespect tradition and courtesy. These families are your staunchest supporters. Without their aid, your ascension to leadership could be challenged. The right mate would stop all of that—"

"I will not be forced into this, Luc. If anyone wants to challenge me for the right to lead, then he or she can face me out in the open. Not hide behind some political game."

"But sire—"

"No. I will not be manipulated. You should know that of me, old friend."

"Yes. Of course." Lucius nodded, placing the hefty envelope on the corner of Xavier's desk.

Vampires did not always inherit the right to lead. Princes were not born but made. Wasn't that what his father had always said? And yet, royal blood flowed in his veins. And it was because of that blood —*his royal DuMont blood*—that so many hungry mamas yearned to tie one of their young to him for eternity.

Fortunately, Xavier had avoided them. He refused to be pressured to take any of the hungry misses for his mate, as of yet. But with his recent ascension, that pressure was now on full keel.

Shit and fuck.

"I've got an idea," Lucius said, thrusting a copy of *The Nightly News* at him.

"What is it, Luc? I am in no mood."

"Read there," his friend said, pointing at an article on the bottom left.

"A retreat? I haven't been on one of those since I was ninety."

"Yes, but remember the fun? I brought my *sheep* at the time, and you pouted because I wouldn't share her!"

"As I recall, she came quite willingly to my bed when summoned, Luc. Why do they still call them sheep? My gods, that is positively medieval!" he replied.

"In case normals see the newspaper, of course."

"Impossible. The Covens bespelled the paper to only go to supes."

"It has happened, Xavier. You know this as well as I."

"True. And Luc, I am sorry about Temple. That was your donor at the time, was it not?"

"Temple? Yes. Not to worry, sire. You always did woo the ladies without trying. Besides, now they have their own donors on hand. You do not need to bring one."

"You don't have to do that, you know."

"What?"

"Calling me sire."

"I do have to call you sire, *sire*. You are my Prince."

"Oh, do shut up. I am your friend, Luc. You've known me my entire life."

"Yes, sire."

"Luc," he growled his friend's name.

"Shall I make the arrangements then?"

"Fine. I will go to this retreat for the weekend if

only to shut you up. And to get away from all this." He indicated the pile of correspondence.

"Very good, sire."

Excerpt from The Enforcer by C.D. Gorri

The moon would soon be full. Isabeau looked at the night sky and pulled the hood of her ivory sweater up over her fiery red curls. She passed between the red and sugar maples, a few tall beech trees, and a lonely pine when a low growl sounded next to her. She reached out to touch the thick fur of the adult she-Wolf who walked beside her through the forest trail.

"It's okay Artemis, let's finish our rounds and get home."

As she walked around the perimeter of her land she chanted an ancient language that few would be able to identify fortifying the wards around her large animal sanctuary. That was what the mortals around her thought it was, and for the most part they were correct.

To them, Isabeau Rose had just arrived in town a few years ago with the deed to five-hundred acres of Northern New Jersey farmland. Within a few months, she'd transformed the abandoned horse farm and the woods around it into a series of habitats for wild animals that were injured or discarded. Creatures that needed a haven for rehabilitation.

She had a main house for herself that boasted ten-bedrooms and six-full baths, an indoor pool and spa, two stables, one for her horses, the other for more exotic wildlife, two large red barns, and a state of the art veterinary clinic on the grounds.

"Out late, aren't you?" Beau turned around to find the source of the unfamiliar voice. She lifted her hand to calm Artemis who was ready to pounce on the intruder.

"Who are you?" she demanded.

"The real question is what are you doing out here so late? Surely your wards don't need reinforcement at this time of night, not out in this quiet New Jersey forest, Sorceress Rose?" The dark stranger spoke with an unearthly calm to his voice that put Beau on edge.

This was no mere mortal. She used her keen

sight to see him despite the darkness and almost gasped aloud. His face was perfect, except for a thin silver scar that ran from his left eyebrow to his chin. His eyes blazed cerulean blue fringed with impossibly dark lashes. They were carefully masked to hide his emotions.

About the Author

C.D. Gorri is a USA Today Bestselling author of steamy paranormal romance and urban fantasy. She is the creator of the Grazi Kelly Universe.

Join her mailing list here: https://www. cdgorri.com/newsletter

An avid reader with a profound love for books and literature, when she is not writing or taking care of her family, she can usually be found with a book or tablet in hand. C.D. lives in her home state of New Jersey where many of her characters or stories are based. Her tales are fast paced yet detailed with satisfying conclusions.

If you enjoy powerful heroines and loyal heroes who face relatable problems in supernatural settings, journey into the Grazi Kelly Universe today. You will find sassy, curvy heroines and sexy, love-driven heroes who find their HEAs between the pages. Werewolves, Bears, Dragons, Tigers, Witches, Romani, Lynxes, Foxes, Thunderbirds, Vampires, and many more Shifters and supernatural creatures dwell within her worlds. The most important thing is every mate in this universe is fated, loyal, and true lovers always get their happily ever afters.

Want to know how it all began? Enter the Grazi Kelly Universe with Wolf Moon: A Grazi Kelly Novel or pick up Charley's Christmas Wolf and dive into the Macconwood Pack Novel Series today.

For a complete list of C.D. Gorri's books visit her website here:

https://www.cdgorri.com/complete-book-list/

Thank you and happy reading!

del mare alla stella,
　　C.D. Gorri

Follow C.D. Gorri here:
　　http://www.cdgorri.com
　　https://www.facebook.com/Cdgorribooks

https://www.bookbub.com/authors/c-d-gorri

https://twitter.com/cgor22

https://instagram.com/cdgorri/

https://www.goodreads.com/cdgorri

https://www.tiktok.com/@cdgorriauthor